The Mirror Diaries: Finding Grace

1

VANESSA COULBECK

GRACE ISN'T SURE WHO SHE IS—or how to feel good in her own skin and embrace the girl she sees in the mirror. Is she the sporty girl who loves competition, like her friend Emma? The smart one with all the answers, like Lilly? Or maybe the effortlessly funny one, like her new friend Anna? And when it comes to showing up with confidence for anything, from tryouts to her new volunteering gig, the questions only get louder. Everyone around her seems to know exactly who they are, but Grace just feels... invisible.

That is, until she finds a mysterious mirror hidden in her attic (yes, really!) and gets a surprise journaling assignment from her teacher that sends her on the ultimate quest. Suddenly, Grace is on a journey she didn't expect: to not only figure out who she is but to learn how to be kinder to the girl she sees in the mirror.

With friendship ups and downs, navigating the pressures of being a young girl, tryouts that test her courage, and some major self-discovery moments (plus a few laugh-out-loud fails), Grace begins to realize that being herself is her true superpower.

For anyone who's ever struggled with body confidence, doubted their worth, or felt the pressure to be "enough," Grace's journey will feel real and relatable. As girls grow and navigate changes in their bodies, emotions, and identity, this journey offers practical, evidence-informed tools and activities focused on self-compassion, empowerment and body image through movement—helping readers build kindness and confidence that go beyond just school and sport

No matter your age, join Grace on this empowering adventure, and discover that being kind to yourself matters just as much as being yourself - and that your greatest superpower is showing up as you, because no one else can.

Text copyright © 2025 by Vanessa Coulbeck / Strong Girl Publishing

Jacket art copyright © 2025 by Strong Girl Publishing

First edition, 2025

ISBN 978-1-0688302-7-3

More Information: StrongGirlPublishing.com

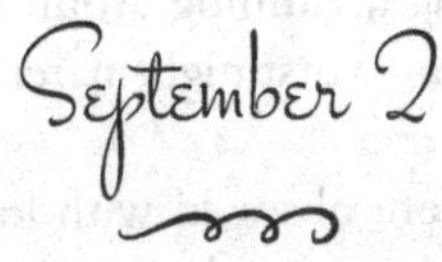

September 2

Dear Diary,

Today was the first day back to school after summer break! When I woke up this morning though, I felt...weird. Nervous, maybe? I couldn't sleep last night because I was so excited. I even picked out my outfit—a blue sundress I got this summer—and even laid out my new shoes I got with my mom back to school shopping last week: the classic white Nike Air Force 1s, still surprised mom let me get these since she doesn't really like the style but I love them.

When I put it on this morning, it felt okay, even though it was like the perfect outfit just yesterday, but suddenly, it seemed like it wasn't quite right. My body feels different from last school year. I have hair on my body, and I think my chest has even started to grow. Maybe. My mom told me that all bodies change as they grow and even when you're an adult your body changes. But it still feels kind of scary, what if I don't like the way I grow? Or if other people don't like how I grow?

I guess I'm not the only one who's nervous about the school year starting. I keep seeing these back to school posts online saying "you're not alone," I think they're talking about being an almost teenager, like it's some kind of club you automatically belong to. Everyone's probably feeling the same way, but still— it's hard to shake the feeling.

When I got to school, everything felt so different. The hallways seemed smaller but louder than they ever have, if that makes sense. I found my best friends Lilly and Emma standing by our lockers talking about basketball tryouts. They're both amazing at sports. Honestly, though, running around in front of everyone every day sounds like my worst nightmare, but I know I'll try my best to cheer them on.

Everyone seems more obsessed with looks this year. It's like every conversation today was about who got taller, who got braces, or who got a new haircut. There was even this weird moment at lunch when Jenny whispered something about Ella's outfit. Ella is new to our school, I met her at camp this summer. But she wasn't even wearing anything weird, in fact I actually really like her outfit. She had tight jean capris on and a flower tank top. Why the comment? I thought about telling her I liked her shirt, but I was afraid that because I liked her outfit, that said something bad about mine.

It's kind of hard not to feel like people are looking at you too —and maybe saying something about what you're wearing. It kind of made me feel weird as I walked into class...I realized my heart was suddenly pounding like crazy.

I snapped out of it when Lilly came to sit beside me at lunch and the first thing she told me was that she loved my dress and wished she could pull a dress like this off as well as I do! I couldn't believe it, why would she want to look like me? It was such a strange feeling. But, then it was class time. This year is definitely going to be a lot more work than last year!

The only part I got really excited about was when our new health teacher, Miss Adler, let us all pick a journal from a big pile of fun, unique notebooks (this is why I am writing in you now, diary!). It was a short class because of a 'welcome back' assembly, so she didn't get to explain much about what we'd be doing this semester, she just said that part of our homework would be keeping a diary. I've tried to since the fourth grade, but it never really stuck—hopefully having it as part of my homework will make me write more. I won't have to hand you in, or anything like that—we'll be submitting our answers in a different notebook or online, so at least no one will read you. I think she might think I'm actually kind of mean if she did... but she did have examples from past students who submitted theirs and were okay with sharing. I'm curious to hear what others at my age last year were going through.

Anyway, that was day one. *Only* day one. I'm sure things will get better—or at least less awkward—as we all figure out how to survive this new school year. Fingers crossed, right?

<h1 style="text-align:center">September 3</h1>

Dear Diary,

Mom kept telling me to hurry up, but I couldn't find my favorite socks (why do socks always disappear?!), and then I spent way too much time trying to decide if my hair looked better in a ponytail or down. I went with the ponytail, but I'm still not sure if that was the right decision. It seems like no matter how I have my hair, I hate it five minutes later. Ugh, sometimes I wish I didn't have hair at all.

Anyway, our first gym class was... an experience. Miss Adler made us run laps today. She said it was to see "where everyone's at," but I'm pretty sure it was just her way of making us sweat before 10 a.m. I guess the ponytail was a good decision.

Lilly and Emma didn't seem to mind—they were racing each other, laughing like it was no big deal. I wish I could enjoy running that much. I can't help but think about everything else. How everyone else seems fine when we're running, but how my legs move, how my breath feels and how my lungs seem to be burning up—it just seems so much harder for me. And I start thinking about how my shorts fit a little differently than Lilly's. She runs so freely, like she's not thinking about any of it. I wish I could feel that way too.

I kept wondering if anyone else noticed. Like, could they see how I felt? Did I look weird? At one point, I thought about faking a stomach ache just to sit on the sidelines, but then Lilly jogged up beside me and said, "You've got this, Grace!" She said it so casually and with a huge grin, like she actually believed it. She's always been so good at being a friend. So I kept trying.

Maybe she wasn't paying attention to all the things I was worrying about. Maybe nobody was. But it's hard to tell your brain to stop when it's so loud, you know?

Later at lunch when I sat with Emma and Lilly, they were talking about school basketball tryouts. Emma told me I should try out for the basketball team. She says I'm more athletic than I think. I don't know about that, but maybe I'll give it a shot just for her.

I couldn't help but feel even more anxious at the thought though: Emma is the queen of the court, Lilly is naturally talented at everything, and I am just Grace. I sometimes like to pass the ball around, but I mostly feel useless and slower than all the other girls so I don't really want to go to tryouts. But I don't want Lilly and Emma to leave me behind and make new friends, so I guess I'll end up going along. Like always.

The rest of the day was fine, I guess. Math was confusing (as usual), and I nearly fell asleep in history. But then I was able to get out of my funk because I had geography class after lunch. I know my friends don't really like it, but I love learning about geography. I think that comes from my mom. She's always telling me these cool facts about other places in the world.

September 4

Dear Diary,

Today felt like a marathon. By the time I got home, I was completely drained, like my brain had been running laps all day instead of my legs. Mom was in the kitchen making one of my favorite dinners: spaghetti! That was a nice surprise. She always knows when I need a little pick-me-up.

She could tell something was up the moment I walked in. She likes to look at people by lowering her reading glasses, which to me defeats the use of glasses, but that's besides the point. It's like her signal that she knows something is going on and she's waiting for me to tell her about it.

She asked me if I'd had a tough day, but I just shrugged and told her not really—it was just weird. She wanted me to explain why, and I hesitated for a second. But I figured, why not tell her? She might get it, she was my age once too. So I told her about gym class yesterday and how I couldn't stop thinking about my legs and how I looked when I ran, and how I'm scared to try out for the basketball team because I'm so slow.

She told me "Grace, do you know what I noticed when you came in just now?"

I had no idea what she was getting at, so I just shook my head.

"That you walked in here with legs that carried you through the whole day. Legs that ran laps, got you to class on time, and brought you home to me." Then she smiled a little and added, "Your legs are amazing, Grace. Not because of how they look, but because of what they let you do."

I didn't really know what to say to that. I mean, I get what she's saying, but it's hard to feel amazing when you're stuck comparing yourself to everyone else. Still, it made me feel a little better, like maybe I was focusing on the wrong things about my body.

Later, we folded laundry and watched Soul Surfer together for our mother/daughter time, our movie night where no boys (dad or my little brother, Jake) are allowed. It's a documentary about Bethany Hamilton, this amazing surfer who lost her arm in a shark attack but still found a way to keep going. She didn't just get back on her board—she competed again. Like, actual surfing competitions. I don't know how she did it. I mean, I freak out over gym class, and she went right back into the ocean after a shark *bit her arm off*. Mom didn't bring up the running thing again tonight, but her words stuck with me anyway.

September 5

Dear Diary,

Friday is my favorite day of the week because it means I get to escape school for a bit and enjoy the weekend. But Fridays also usually mean grades, and today we got our first mini-assignment back of the year. We had to write a "Future Me letter" basically a letter to ourselves about what we hoped for this year, what we were excited (or nervous) about, and what kind of person we wanted to be by the end of this grade.. It was supposed to be an easy grade assignment but I only got a B. A *B!* I usually get all A's, so seeing that letter staring up at me felt like someone had poured cold water over my head. I guess I didn't put as much effort into it as I thought I did. There were only a couple spelling errors, a one sentence structure mistake. I couldn't believe that was enough points to get a B.

Lilly got hers back too, also a B, but she didn't seem nearly as upset as I was. "We'll get better," she said, shrugging like it was no big deal. "It's only the first assignment. Plus, it was a fun activity to do."

For a moment, her calm voice and easy smile made me feel a little better. But how does she stay so positive all the time? It's like nothing gets to her.

And then there's Emma. She got an A, of course, but instead of being happy about it, she said, "Ugh, I was so close to an A+."

Seriously? I couldn't even imagine being upset about that. She's so good at everything—writing, math, sports, life—it's like she's on a completely different level than me. Whatever, at least Lilly understood.

When the final bell rang, I felt this huge wave of relief wash over me. I could finally leave school behind and just breathe. Mom texted to say she's making lasagna and Caesar salad which is my all time favorite dinner, and for a second, I felt excited. But then that little voice in my head crept in, reminding me of how I've been feeling lately.

I don't know why, but my favourite foods don't feel as exciting anymore. The lunch talk at school this year seems to be about what people are eating or really, what they are not eating. Emma was talking about how balanced her meal was, with just the right mix of protein, veggies, and carbs. One girl mentioned she's cutting out dairy, another said she's trying vegetarian meals. No one's saying you *have* to eat a certain way, but it's like everyone is thinking about it. I nodded along, but it made me wonder about my own eating habits. Does it mean my favourite foods are not good enough? Because now when I see Emma, I start thinking about how different we look. She seems so strong and confident. I wish I could feel that way too, does food have anything to do with that?

I tried to push the thoughts away, but they stuck to me like gum on the bottom of my shoe. Why can't I just feel okay for once? It's like there's an invisible weight pressing down on me.

I wish I could go back to the days when I didn't think about these things. When I could just be myself without comparing everything to everyone else.

Future Me Letter Assignment

1. Who am I right now?

Right now, I'm someone who's still figuring things out. I sometimes doubt myself, but I know I have a lot to offer. I love writing, but I'm not always confident in my work. I can be shy around new people, but when I'm comfortable, I'm a good listener and a caring friend. I want to work on being more confident in who I am, not second-guessing myself so much.

2. What are my hopes for this school year?

I hope to grow in confidence. I want to speak up more in class and not be afraid to show who I really am. I hope to make at least one new close friend and be a better listener and supporter to the friends I already have. I also want to try new things, like joining a club or something creative, to see if I can discover something I'm really passionate about.

3. Who do I want to become?

By the end of the year, I want to be someone who is not afraid to stand up for herself and others. I want to be the girl who can walk into a room and feel like she belongs, without worrying what others think. I want to be confident in my talents, whether it's writing or something else. I want to be the kind of person who lifts others up and doesn't let self-doubt get in the way.

4. What am I excited to try this year?

I'm excited to try new activities and maybe even join a club or sports team. I want to explore my creative side more and see if there's something else I'm really passionate about. I'm also excited to learn more about myself, especially by stepping out of my comfort zone and trying things I wouldn't normally do.

5. What challenges do I think I might face?

I think I'll struggle with staying confident, especially when things don't go as planned. I also worry about fitting in and whether I'm doing enough. I might have days when I feel like I'm not measuring up to others or that I'm falling behind. I know I'll need to remind myself that it's okay to not be perfect.

6. How will I handle those challenges?

I don't know what I'll do. I haven't done a very good job at being confident so far.

7. What is one thing I want to remember every day?

To do my homework.

8. Here's a few sentences to my future self.

Dear Future Me,
I hope you're proud of how far you've come this year. I hope you've stayed true to yourself and faced challenges with courage. I hope you've made new friends, stepped out of your comfort zone, and found something you're passionate about. No matter what, remember you are enough just as you are. Keep growing, keep learning, and keep being the amazing person I know you're becoming.

FROM THE DESK OF MISS ADLER

Dear Grace,

Thank you for sharing your letter! It's clear that you've put a lot of thought into your goals for this year, and I appreciate how honest you've been about who you are right now. You've done a great job of reflecting on your hopes for personal growth, like building your confidence and stepping outside your comfort zone. I really like the vision you have for yourself at the end of the year—someone who's confident and able to stand up for both herself and others.

That said, I noticed that some sections were left incomplete or like you didn't quite finish your thoughts, and I think filling these in could help you clarify your goals and make them even more powerful. For example, when you talk about handling challenges, it would be helpful to think about some strategies you might use when things don't go as planned. What steps can you take to stay calm and confident? And for your "One thing I want to remember every day," rather than something that's a task on your schedule, it might be more helpful to pick a mantra or affirmation that will remind you of your worth and your goals. This could be something simple, like "I am enough, and I am doing my best." We will be working on this throughout the new school year, so don't worry that you haven't thought of one yet!

You've got a lot of great ideas, Grace, and I think with just a little more detail, this letter can become a really strong tool for tracking your growth this year.

Grade: B – Strong reflection with some unfinished thoughts. Keep working on filling out the blanks to make your goals even more clear and actionable.

Keep up the good work!

-Miss Adler

September 6

Dear Diary,

Mom made pancakes this morning, it made the whole house smell warm and buttery. She even let me flip some of the pancakes, even though some of them were lopsided (okay, one was a full-on blob), but Mom said they all taste the same anyway.

After breakfast, I went to the park with Emma and Lilly. We brought a basketball and started a game of Horse. Surprise, surprise, I lost. But Lilly said she saw someone say online today, "You don't have to be the best to belong. You're part of the team just because you show up." Lilly is always quoting random motivational things she sees online! It's nice, but I'm not sure I believe that. Basketball tryouts are officially next week and my brain has been doing cartwheels over it. I mean, how can I belong when I'm not fast like the other girls? What happens if I try out and don't make the team? Is that better than if I don't try out at all?

Lilly told me she's nervous too, but we can just practice our way out of it. "We're all going to feel nervous if we don't practice together, so let's just go for it!" she said.

I don't know about that. For one thing, I don't think Emma even gets nervous. She's like a superhero on the court. But Lilly is really trying to convince me to at least try, and maybe she's right but I feel so sure I'll fail. I've been in my head all week thinking about how I should not even be practicing to try out because all the other girls are faster, more agile, and have more stamina than me. But I said I would try out for the basketball team... so I am going to just practice with Emma and Lilly and try my best.

I got so caught up in my thoughts that I barely noticed a ball whiz past my head. I turned just in time to see the three most popular girls in our class, Miranda, Jenny, and Katy strolling by, giggling about how they nearly hit me in the head. My stomach twisted into a knot. They can be such mean girls. I thought about hitting them back with a ball, but I knew I would miss. How annoying! Maybe I should try to be good at basketball just so I can throw a ball back at them and land it.

Thinking about it now, I've realized something about them. It's not just what they say, it's how they make me feel about myself. Like, somehow the way I look isn't okay. I think that's why I really don't like tryouts or gym class. The idea of changing in front of others makes me want to disappear. I always wear leggings and a long-sleeve shirt or at least a t-shirt because I feel more comfortable that way. Sometimes, I wish I could wear tank tops and shorts like Emma without worrying so much.

September 8

Dear Diary,

Miss Adler decided to set aside some free gym space time for us to practice before the tryouts. If you weren't trying out, that was okay too, you could just play for fun. And everyone seemed to really enjoy themselves—except me. As expected, I did not run fast enough or get any baskets, and I let my team down by missing all the free throws (you know, that shot you have to do when someone fouls you) because I felt like everyone was staring at me while I was about to shoot the ball.

I kept noticing how easily Emma moved through the drills and I was so jealous. She made it look so effortless, while I struggled to keep up. My arms felt like jelly by the third round of passing, and I tripped over my own feet during a layup attempt. Lilly cheered me on anyway, saying, "You're getting faster, Grace!" even though I wasn't. Maybe I should give those affirmations that Miss Adler assigned us after gym class a shot—she said this year, we're really focusing on getting to know ourselves and working on our mental health and body image. She swears that affirmations work, even if they feel silly at first. I guess I'll give it a try.

THE POWER OF AFFIRMATIONS

As a class, create a list of positive affirmations. Each student should write down at least three things they appreciate about their body. (Think about functionality here versus superficial). Share one of these affirmations with a partner or the class. Put these affirmations somewhere you'll see them and repeat these affirmations daily.

Your Affirmations:

1. My body is strong and capable.

2. I am proud of everything my body does for me.

3. I am enough, just as I am.

I'm back! So, it felt weird. Like, major cringe. But also kind of freeing? I looked in the bathroom mirror where I always feel all of my insecurities. I tried saying that I am enough, and that my body is strong and capable. And I even added a new one, "I am more than my appearance. I am strong for showing up." I wrote it on a sticky note and stuck it to my bathroom mirror. I'll admit to you, Diary, that I followed up in my head with, "even though I felt horrible in the moment." But I didn't think Miss Adler would appreciate me saying that out loud or writing it down.

I don't normally talk to myself like that, but maybe that's the point? I need to be nice to myself and talk to myself that way. It didn't feel natural, but it didn't feel bad, either.

And a few minutes later, when I was thinking back to practice, I did remember one positive moment where Emma cheered me on like I'd made the winning shot, even when I missed again. Miss Adler pointed at the slogan written on the wall in the gym that says, "You miss 100% of the shots you don't take." And Lilly actually said, "Anyway, the more you miss, the closer you get to making one. Trust me!" I did roll my eyes at her, but it made me smile after. So maybe the affirmations gave me a little positive boost to bring that memory up.

Goodnight, Diary. Tomorrow is a new day!

September 10

Dear Diary,

Miss Adler had us write three things we appreciate about our bodies today—not how they look, but what they *do* for us. She called it an exercise in gratitude, but right away, my brain went straight to all the things I don't like, like how my hair frizzes up in gym class, or how I wish my legs looked the way they do in my head, or even how I wish my teeth were straighter.

Miss Adler walked around the room and said, "Remember, your body is your teammate, not your competition. Think about all the things it does for you every day, without even needing to be told." Then she said something that really stuck with me: "And don't forget, you're still growing. Your body is changing all the time. Try to appreciate where it is now, not just where you think it 'should' or 'could' be."

She even shared her own list to help us get started. "I'm grateful that my legs carry me through the day, that my heart keeps beating without me having to think about it, and that I have the energy to play with my kids," she said. It made sense, but it still felt kind of silly, like when I did those affirmations. But seriously, when was the last time I appreciated my body for what it can do instead of how it looks?

It took me a minute, but I managed to come up with this list.

1. My legs let me run, even if I'm slow sometimes.
2. My hands help me draw and write.
3. My lungs let me breathe deep when I'm nervous, like in gym class.

Then Miss Adler asked us to share one thing from our list. I was paired with Lilly, thank goodness, and I could tell Lilly was nervous about sharing too. Lilly said she appreciates her arms because they're strong and let her play basketball. I told her about my legs and how they carry me through the day, even when I'm tired. She smiled and said, "That's a good one. Your legs are strong, Grace. I've seen you run—and you're not slow, you just think you are!"

But we weren't the only nervous ones about sharing. Ella raised her hand and said she was having trouble coming up with even one thing. Miss Adler reassured her, saying, "It's okay to struggle with this at first. It takes practice to think about our bodies positively. Start small, and it'll grow." By the end of the class, Ella said she appreciated that her legs walk her to school every day. That was a really good one. I saw Jenny look like she was about to make some kind of mean comment, but luckily, she didn't say anything.

Miss Adler told us to repeat these affirmations to ourselves every day, even if it feels silly, and the best time to do it is first thing when we wake up in the morning. "The more you remind yourself of the good things, the easier it gets to believe them," she said.

Maybe she's right. It felt kind of nice to think about my body as something good for once. Who knows? I might even add a few new things to my list.

Dear Diary,

Today was so scary. It started with basketball tryouts, which was first thing in the morning, before school even started. At least I know I will get to sleep-in tomorrow since it's Saturday. I tried saying my affirmations when I woke up. It really does feel ridiculous but I might as well give it a fair shot, and I could use all the help I could get for tryouts. They are definitely going to take some getting used to, but I really want to believe that I am a strong and capable person.

Anyway, on to tryouts. I was still pretty not excited about doing them, but I promised Lilly and Emma that I would, so I showed up because I didn't want to be totally left out. At least if I didn't make the team, I could say it wasn't my fault, but if I didn't bother, I was worried they'd judge me for that. Mr. Moonstone was the first person I saw when I got dropped off, he had his clipboard and was looking really official. Mr. Moonstone is our history teacher and also my school's main basketball coach. He's a little scary. I assumed the clipboard had everyone's names so he could check off what we did right and wrong and I was worried that he'd run out of room in the 'wrong' column for me! I was one of the first kids there, but the other students started trickling in quickly, including Emma and Lilly. There wasn't any time to really talk to them before it got started though. It felt like out of nowhere, the 60 minute buzzer started for the tryout, which was basically just four ten-minute sets of free play with random teams. I could see that Emma was on fire, nailing every layup and foul shot like she was born to play. Lilly wasn't the best, but she was such a good teammate that I could see Mr. Moonstone nodding approvingly at her.

For me, the tryout went just like the practice did: I couldn't even land a basket and I couldn't catch the ball anytime someone tried to pass it to me. I felt so embarrassed, I was hot and sweaty and it seemed like everyone's eyes were on me. I don't know if I can do that again, and there are still a couple more to get through!

At lunch, all the boys couldn't stop talking about how good Emma is, saying stuff like, "Emma's a beast on the court," (That was Graham, he is super cute.) Emma soaked up the compliments (which, to be fair, she totally deserved), but Lilly and I just sat there. I tried not to care, but it's hard not to compare myself when Emma seems to have everything together. Lilly and I were excited for her. But a part of me felt sad because Emma seems to always get the attention from boys and I never have any of them talk to me. It'd be nice to have some attention that feels good, you know?

I guess Jenny caught me staring because she said to me, "Oh Grace, I'm sure once you can land a basket, the boys will be all over you." Then she smirked, and I could tell she was thinking, "Not that that's likely to ever happen."

Diary, I don't know what's happening. Now it feels like this weird competition—on and off the court. Who's the best, who looks the best, who gets the most attention. It doesn't even feel like it's about our basketball talent anymore, it feels like it's about everything.

I want to be excited for Emma, and I *am*. But why does it feel like every win of hers makes me shrink a little smaller? Why does everything feel so complicated now?

Maybe tomorrow will be better. I hope it will.

September 15

Dear Diary,

Today, Miss Adler had us do an activity to log our emotions over the past week. She said it was important to reflect on how we're feeling, but honestly, I wasn't sure I wanted to sum up everything swirling around in my head. When I mentioned that I already write in you a lot, Diary, Miss Adler's face lit up like I'd just told her I won the lottery. "Grace, you're setting yourself up for greatness." Greatness? I don't know about that. Most of the time, writing feels like dragging my feelings out into the open, and I'm not always sure I want to look at them. But other times, it's like talking to a best friend who I know won't judge me.

But maybe Miss Adler has a point. It usually does make me feel better just to get my thoughts out of my head. She said journaling helps build confidence. Could it really work? But, Diary, you'll never believe what happened next. At lunch, Emma and Lilly both admitted they were writing often in their journals too! Emma said she's mostly been writing when she's stressed about a game, and Lilly uses hers for drawing or jotting down things that make her happy—but still. It made me feel a little less... alone, I guess. We even talked about maybe sharing some of the things we've written. At first, the idea terrified me. What if they see the parts where I write about feeling like I don't belong or not being good enough? But then Lilly said, "Sharing could help us cheer each other on, just like we do at practice."

Emma added, "Yeah, and maybe it'll help us get out of our own heads sometimes. I know I overthink stuff a lot."

I never imagined *Emma* overthinking anything. She always seems so cool and collected. But maybe there's more to her than I see, even though I've known her forever.So now, I'm both nervous and kind of excited. What if sharing our journals really does help us feel closer? What if it makes us stronger, like a real team, even off the court?

I'll think about it. For now, I guess I'll keep writing like Miss Adler suggested. Maybe this is what she meant about greatness—finding little ways to be brave.

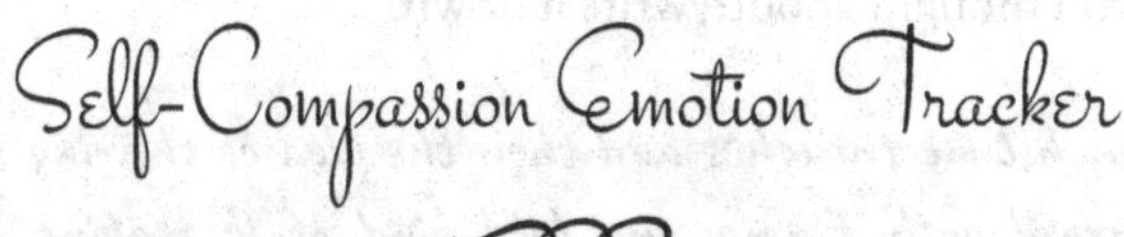

Self-Compassion Emotion Tracker

This worksheet helps you understand and care for your emotions. It's okay to feel however you feel—there's no right or wrong way to feel. Practice being kind to yourself as you explore your feelings.

How Are You Feeling Right Now? Choose the emotion(s) that best describe how you feel. You can underline or write your own.

Happy Anxious Angry Sad Excited Frustrated Embarrassed Worried Confident Surprised Confused Tired Proud <u>Nervous</u>
Other: _________

How Strong Is the Emotion? On a scale from 1 to 10, how strong is this emotion for you right now? 1 is a little bit, and 10 is a lot.

7/10

. . .

What Happened to Make You Feel This Way? Think about what triggered this emotion. Was it a person, a situation, or something you thought about? Write it down.

Lunch time thoughts and then the idea of sharing my journal with Emma and Lilly kind of is making me question if I actually would want them to know what I've been thinking. It's scary because what if they read the parts where I feel insecure or not good enough? But I also want to trust them.

How Did Your Body Feel? How did your body react when you felt this emotion? Did your heart race, did you feel tense, or did you feel calm? This helps you understand how your emotions show up physically.

When I think about sharing my journal, my stomach feels kind of tight, and my heart beats a little faster. It's like a mix of nerves and excitement. When I heard the lunch talk, I started to feel a little self-conscious. My shoulders got tense, and I felt a little anxious.

Kindness to Yourself: Take a deep breath. It's okay to feel this way. Write something kind to yourself about this emotion, like you would tell a friend who feels the same way. Examples: "It's okay to feel upset," or "I'm proud of myself for noticing how I feel."

Writing about my emotions doesn't make me weak—it means I'm learning more about myself. I'm brave for trying something new. And as for lunch? I can't let other people's choices make me doubt mine. My body is strong and capable, and it deserves food that makes me feel good.

What Could You Do to Be Kind to Yourself Right Now? What is one thing you can do to help yourself feel better or comfort yourself? It could be something small like taking deep breaths, talking to someone you trust, or doing something fun.

I can take a few deep breaths and remind myself that sharing my feelings might actually help me connect with Emma and Lilly. Or I can just tell them I'm not ready to share my journal. Either way, I'll be okay. I can also remind myself that I don't need to compare my food choices to anyone else's. I'm doing my best, and that's enough.

How Would You Like to Feel? Think about how you would like to feel now. You can keep the same emotion or choose a new one. What would help you feel more peaceful or happy?

I'd like to feel confident and open. I want to trust myself and my friends more, even when I'm nervous. I'll feel better once I remember that they're my team. I want to stop comparing my food choices to others' and just focus on what makes me feel good.

. . .

Self-Compassion Practice: Write or draw something that helps you feel better or shows self-compassion. It could be a quote, an affirmation, or something you like doing to feel calm. You can also practice deep breathing or self-soothing activities.

I can remind myself that it's okay to be vulnerable. "It's okay to feel how I feel. I'm enough, just as I am." I could also try writing out some positive affirmations for myself, like "I am brave," and "I am worthy of love and support." And for my lunch, I'll say, "I'm nourishing my body in the way it needs today."

September 17

Dear Diary,

Tonight, we went to my parents' friends' house for a BBQ and swim night. As usual, I was on Jake duty—and because they also have a little kid, I was sort of babysitting. The two of them together are pure chaos! Last time, they decided the basement carpet needed a crayon makeover... and guess who had to clean it up? Me. (Because I was too distracted on FaceTime with Lilly to notice it happening.)

Getting ready was its own ordeal. I wanted to wear my favorite bathing suit, but of course, I couldn't find it anywhere. I tore through my drawers, getting more and more annoyed, until Mom walked in, took one look at my disaster of a room, and casually tossed the suit at me. "Maybe if you cleaned up once in a while, you'd actually know where your stuff is," she said with that *Mom look*. Ugh. She had a point, but still.

Before we left, Dad tried to lighten the mood with one of his classic dad jokes. I rolled my eyes, but secretly, I do love how corny he is sometimes.

When we got there, I had to stay on high alert. Jake and his little partner-in-crime wasted no time turning the couch into their superhero headquarters, leaping from cushion to cushion. I had to step in before one of them actually learned to fly. Just as I was reaching my limit, Dad swooped in with a grin and said something like "Looks like the superhero sidekicks need a little supervision tonight." Thank goodness! All I wanted to do was swim since they have a pool, and we finally got to after dinner. The pool was exactly what I needed. I couldn't help but laugh when Jake attempted a cannonball but belly-flopped instead. And since none of my friends were there, I didn't think twice about how I looked in my bathing suit, I just had fun splashing around like a little kid.

By the time we left, I was completely wiped out. But at least this time, there was no carpet "art" to clean up and I got a swim out of it.

September 18

Dear Diary,

It was so weird: I didn't feel like eating my lunch today. In fact, I noticed a lot of the girls weren't eating their lunches. This isn't the first time I've seen it, but today felt like almost everyone was pushing their food around their trays or just not bothering at all. Even Emma, who used to be the queen of eating whatever she wanted without a second thought, left her sandwich untouched. I asked her about it, she said, "I have to be careful now that I'm on the team. Gotta stay in shape."

I guess Emma would know how to take care of her body if she got on the team. But it didn't sound like the Emma I know. Emma, who once proudly devoured an entire pizza after practice because, as she said, "athletes need their fuel."

Speaking of the team, Emma and Lilly both managed to get placed on the team since the tryout, and of course, I didn't make a placement. I don't know why I didn't tell you that before—I guess I was a little embarrassed and just didn't want to even write it down because then I'd have to think about it. We did get an email that explained that there's going to be more practice sessions offered for students who didn't get placed so that maybe we could make the team for the winter session. I'm not sure if I want to go through that again.

Anyway. Back to lunch. When I looked at what I had

brought to school today—a peanut butter and jelly sandwich, an apple, and a juice box—suddenly, it felt like too much. And it felt like such an immature meal, like one a little kid would have. Is it lame that it's my favorite? Everyone else's trays were empty because they didn't get food or they barely touched the food they did get. If they didn't need lunch to get through the day, then maybe I didn't either?

But then Mom's voice echoed in my head. She told me once, "Your body is like a car, Grace. Without fuel, it won't run." And yet, the girls who skip lunch seem to do just fine in school, so maybe she's wrong? Maybe I don't need food as much as she says I do. But my stomach was growling, so I ate my sandwich even though I felt like everyone was watching me and judging me. The rest of lunch felt weird, I couldn't finish my apple. Lilly noticed, of course. She always does. She didn't say anything, but she gave me that look, the one that says she knows something's up. (Lilly finished her entire lunch, and chatted away happily the whole time like she didn't notice anything weird. I wish I could be as chill as her.)

September 19

Dear Diary,

Mom has been asking me to help with her volunteer work now that I'm old enough to be a junior volunteer. I'm not sure how I feel about it yet—it's definitely a lot when I already feel like dealing with school is overwhelming.

And it's not really easy work either. She helps kids who are dealing with really serious illnesses, like cancer and heart conditions. This month has been especially busy because it's almost cancer awareness month, so there have been a lot of fundraisers and events being planned.

But since I'm not playing basketball, I do have some free time where Emma and Lilly aren't around to hang out, so I guess I should do something so I don't seem like such a loser. It's embarrassing when they have all this stuff going on and I'm just home alone. So when she asked if I wanted to come with her this weekend, I wasn't excited about it, but I said yes so I could tell Emma and Lilly I was busy.

Mom also said we're going to be giving away some of our things to help families who need support right now. She asked me to go through my closet and pick out clothes or books to give away, but honestly, it's hard to think about letting go of some of my stuff. Some of my favorite things are in there, and they mean a lot to me. But Mom told me that sometimes we get so focused on our own worries that we forget to notice the good things we already have. She told me about how some families are struggling just to get through each day, and it made me think about the kids that Mom is always talking about. Some of them spend so much time in hospitals, and they don't get to do the things I do everyday, like going to school or playing with friends. So I pulled out a few things to give away, and even though it makes me sad that I won't have them anymore, I did feel a little lighter when I put them all in the box labeled 'donations' that Mom had by the door.

I'm still feeling a little unsure about tomorrow, but I think I'm starting to understand why Mom cares so much about helping others. It's not about giving up things—it's about sharing what we can to make someone else's life a little better.

Goodnight, Diary. Wish me luck tomorrow.

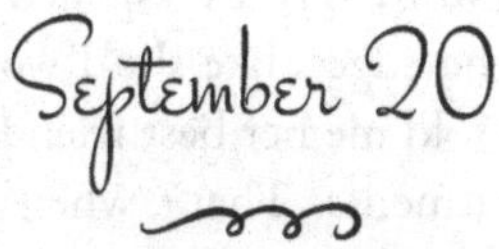

Dear Diary,

Today was my first day volunteering with Mom's charity, and to be honest, I wasn't exactly excited about it at all this morning. In fact, I almost pretended to feel sick so I could stay in the car. But then I met Anna.

The first thing I noticed about her was her outfit—she was wearing bright yellow overalls covered in doodles, like someone had drawn all over them with markers. Later, I found out she had done the drawings herself. "Boring clothes are no fun," she said when I asked about them. "Why not turn them into something you love?"

She was about my age and had purple streaks in her hair and these chunky sneakers with mismatched laces—one neon green and the other hot pink. She looked like she'd stepped out of an art supply store, and I couldn't help but be curious. Also, a little jealous. Mom would never let me get highlights!

We were paired up to sort donation bins, and she introduced herself right away. "Hey, I'm Anna," she said, holding out her hand like we were about to make a business deal. When I told her my name, she smiled and said, "Grace is a solid name. You don't meet many Graces these days."

I wasn't sure what to say to her at first. She seemed so confident and comfortable in her own skin, which was kind of intimidating. But then she started cracking jokes about how we were basically the "junk inspectors," and before I knew it, we were laughing like old friends.

At one point, I noticed the bracelet on her wrist—a simple woven band with the word "HOPE" spelled out in beads. It was a little frayed around the edges, like she'd worn it forever. I asked her about it, and she told me her best friend made it for her back when she started treatments. That's when I realized she wasn't just another volunteer—she was part of the community Mom's charity was helping.

But here's the thing, Diary: Anna didn't seem like someone who was sick. She seemed like someone who was just really, fully *living*. After she told me about her bracelet, she told me that people always want to focus on what's wrong with you, but that she likes to focus on what's right. It really shifted my thinking. I've spent so much time lately in my head obsessing over things like if I look weird when I run, if people at school think I'm cool, or if I should eat my lunch. But here was Anna, making the best of everything, even when things weren't easy for her. I didn't ask her what kind of treatments she needed, and she didn't tell me. But it was okay. I figured she would tell me if she wanted me to know.

By the end of the day, she'd convinced me to add a few doodles to her overalls. She handed me a marker and said, "Come on, Grace, leave your mark!" I drew a tiny star on the pocket, and she grinned like I'd just painted a masterpiece.

Meeting Anna made me think that maybe this volunteering thing won't be so bad after all.

September 21

Dear Diary,

I only met Anna yesterday, but she already feels like someone I've known forever. I was actually excited to get back to volunteering this morning! She's so funny and easy to talk to, like the kind of friend you don't have to try so hard around.

Today, she asked me to follow her on TikTok, and oh my gosh, her videos are *hilarious*. She makes these silly dance videos in the hospital with the nurses and even the doctors sometimes. One of them is this weird robot dance where she's wearing her hospital gown and those fuzzy socks they give you. It was so funny I almost snorted my juice.

She told me "dancing's the best way to forget you're stuck in the hospital." I asked her if it's hard to be here so much, and she shrugged like it was no big deal. "I mean, yeah, sometimes," she said. "So, I just dance. It makes me feel better."

I didn't know what to say. I mean, if I were stuck in the hospital all the time, I'd probably cry nonstop. But she was just smiling at me like it was the easiest thing in the world to think that way. How did she get to be so strong?

Then I told her I've been having a hard time at school lately, not really feeling like I fit in. I didn't think she would care about my problems, they felt so small and trivial compared to what she was going through, but she said, "Grace, everyone feels like that sometimes. You just have to find the people who like you for *you*. The rest doesn't matter."

I don't know how she does it—being so calm about stuff. I told her I think about what other people think of me a lot, and she said "Well, it's not like their opinions make you any cooler or less cool. Just be yourself. It feels a lot better to do what I like anyways." She made it sound so easy, but I think she's braver than me.

Oh, and guess what? She wants me to make a TikTok with her at the next event. She said we can do a funny one where we pretend to be old ladies at a tea party. I'm kind of nervous—I've never been in a TikTok before—but Anna said that it's supposed to be fun, and to stop thinking about everything so much!

I think she's right. She makes everything seem like it doesn't have to be so serious. I don't know how she does it, but I want to be more like her.

September 23

Dear Diary,

In health class today, Miss Adler handed out a sheet titled the "Body Appreciation Map." Everyone groaned. We already did this a while ago! Why should we have to do it again? But she said she'd been hearing students after gym class complaining about their bodies, so she wanted us to do it again. "It's not a one and done thing," she said. "Body appreciation can take a lot of work."

Anyway, we're supposed to start by writing down three things we like about our body, things we do well, or things we appreciate about the way our body works for us... and we have to do it every day for a week. I just wanted to roll my eyes at it.

But then I thought about Anna. She'd probably laugh about how hard it is to pick just three things, but she'd actually mean it. I realized as we were working our way through the donation piles that Anna has trouble doing things I take for granted. At the end of volunteering on Sunday, she admitted to me that it can be hard for her to keep up when her body feels so tired all the time. But she still dances, still smiles, still jokes about stuff most people wouldn't.

So, when I stared at my blank chart, I decided to write these three things:

1. My legs, because they let me run and play basketball
   (even if I'm not the fastest).
2. My hands, because they hold a pencil so I can write
   this chart.
3. My laugh, because Anna says I have a good one, and
   maybe she's right.

It felt weird just like last time, like I was bragging or something, especially knowing that Anna can't do so much. But Miss Adler kept reminding us it's about realizing what we *can* do, not just what I (or others) can't.

I don't know if I'll do this every single day, but Miss Adler's advice has been right so far, so maybe this will work too.

September 25

Dear Diary,

Miss Adler asked us all to bring in our journals this morning, and I thought, *Okay, no big deal. She won't read them out loud.* But guess what? She did!

Well, for a second I thought she did—she didn't share anyone's name, and the entries she read were from last year's class. Hearing those entries... it was like someone cracked open a window and let all our hidden feelings out into the room. I couldn't believe it. So many girls felt the same way I do—unsure about their bodies, nervous about being judged, and even scared to join in on things because of how they look.

The room was silent when she stopped reading, like we were all holding our breath. It was sad, but also comforting in this strange way. I mean, I'm not *alone*. None of us are. I think it was silent because it was so sad but so powerful and comforting at the same time. I did not realize how many of my classmates were also struggling with the changes in their body shape and size. Also that they shy away from playing sports because of the way their bodies look and how they feel. I didn't realize that we're all so mean to ourselves.

One of the entries sounded like it could've been Emma's, but it definitely was just someone from last year. It talked about being an athlete and feeling all this pressure to look a certain way, like being strong wasn't enough, she had to be pretty too. It hit me: maybe that's why Emma's been skipping lunch lately. I always thought she had everything figured out, but maybe she's struggling, too, just like the rest of us. When the bell rang, everyone was still kind of quiet. Like we didn't know what to say.

I walked straight over to Lilly and Emma, and we headed outside for recess. A few other girls joined us, and after a few awkward minutes, we started to talk about what Miss Adler had read in class. For the first time, it felt like we weren't just talking —we were *really* listening to each other.

I decided to share my sticky note with them. You know, the one with the positive words I've been practicing. "I am more than my appearance. I am strong for showing up." It felt a little scary to say it out loud, but the way the other girls nodded and smiled made me think, *Maybe this actually works.*

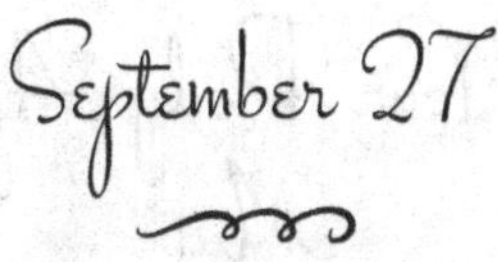

September 27

Dear Diary,

Miss Adler told us she's bringing in a guest speaker to talk about self-compassion later this week. I've never heard of it before, but it sounds interesting? I mean, I see stuff like affirmations and stuff like self-love hacks on TikTok and Instagram, but I've never really believed they could work for me. Who knows? Maybe it'll help me feel better, even just a little.

She also gave us some homework: This body appreciation map. She said it'll help start the conversation when Stella—the speaker—shows up. Hmm.

Creating Your Body Appreciation Map

This exercise helps us focus on what our bodies do for us, not just how they look. It's a way to be kind and thankful to ourselves for all the amazing things our bodies help us with every day! Draw yourself in any way you like, label parts of your body, and think about what you appreciate about each part based on what it helps you do.

Draw Yourself: Start by drawing yourself! You can draw yourself however you want—just a simple outline or a detailed picture. Don't worry about it being perfect; it's all about how you see yourself.

Label Your Body Parts: After you draw yourself, label the different parts of your body. You can choose to label parts like your head, arms, legs, hands, feet, heart, eyes, hair, stomach, and more. It's up to you! Use arrows or lines to point to each part of your body.

Think About What Each Part Does: Now, look at each part you labeled and think about what it helps you do. For example, your arms help you hug, your legs help you run, your stomach helps you digest food, etc.

Write down what you appreciate about each body part and how it helps you in your everyday life. You can use the following prompts to help you:

- I appreciate my ___ because it helps me ___.
- My ___ helps me ___ and I'm thankful for that because ___.

Reflection: Once you've filled in the chart for each body part, take a moment to look at everything you've written. Think about how all your body parts work together to help you do amazing things every day. You can even share with the class or a friend what body part you appreciate the most and why.

I appreciate my eyes because they help me see my favorite things, like books and my pets
I appreciate my arms because they help me hug my friends and lift things I need
I appreciate my hands because they help me draw and write, and give high fives
I appreciate my legs because they help me run and jump, especially when I play sports

<h1 style="text-align:center">September 28</h1>

Dear Diary,

This morning felt so different. The sun was shining through the windows like it was the middle of summer, even though it's fall. I could hear music blasting through the house, and Mom was up early, making pancakes with extra syrup. Jake was making his usual grumpy noises, but I was feeling something else—something exciting.

Mom called for us to go upstairs and help her pull out more stuff to donate, and I followed her to the attic. I'd never been up there before. Jake always tells me stories about the "things" that live in the attic—he says things *appear* and then disappear, but I wasn't scared. Everyone was up there, so I felt safe.

It was dusty and a little musty in the attic, and there were piles of old boxes everywhere. It looked like a place where time just stood still, where things get forgotten. But then, in the corner of the room, hidden behind some boxes, I spotted something shiny. It was a mirror! But not like the ones we see every day. This one was a small handheld mirror with a beautiful flowery frame with swirly engravings that made it look magical.

The weirdest part was a sticky note on it. The handwriting looked kind of like a combination of mine and my Mom's.

I picked up the sticky note, and can you believe it? It said, "Daily Affirmation: Being myself is my superpower." How wild is that? And when I looked in the mirror at myself, it was like something clicked. Instead of seeing my usual reflection—my messy hair, the freckles on my nose, or the way I squint when I smile—I saw... more. I saw myself, but in a way that made me feel *good*. Like I was worth something beyond just how I looked on the outside. I still looked the same, but different somehow.

My heart started racing with excitement. I couldn't stop staring. For the first time, I didn't hear that voice in my head saying, "You're not enough" or "You could do better." It just felt quiet—and warm.

This mirror felt like a new secret treasure, something just for me and for seeing myself in a new way.

Mom was calling for me to come help with the boxes, but I couldn't stop thinking about the mirror and how good I felt looking in it. I want to hold onto this feeling! I brought down the boxes of stuff that were going to the donation bin, but I put the mirror in my room. It had to mean something, finding a sticky note just like the one I had on my mirror!

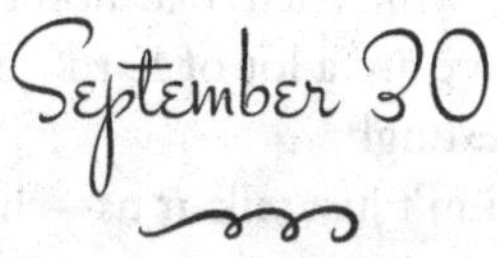

Dear Diary,

Today in class, something really interesting happened. Miss Adler introduced us to Stella, the guest speaker to talk about self compassion and body image. She seemed really cool—she just graduated from a PhD program so she's really smart, but she didn't seem old like most of the teachers. (Sorry, Miss Adler!) She seemed more like us, and she sounded more like us too. You know, less like a teacher and more like a friend or an older cousin or something. She seemed to really get what we were going through, especially the girls.

Before she came, I didn't know what to expect from her. When Miss Adler told us she was coming, I figured it might just be another one of those talks where they tell us we should "love ourselves" but don't actually show us how.

But that wasn't the case. Stella talked to us about just how much pressure there is—especially for us girls—to look a certain way. Like, we're constantly surrounded by these images of what we're *supposed* to look like. On social media. In ads. Even in sports. Everyone's always talking about abs or glow-ups or what workouts they're doing. And yeah, maybe boys have their own insecurities too—especially after hearing some of those anonymous notes Miss Adler read out loud the other day—but it doesn't help when they're always complimenting us only on our looks or bodies. It just adds to the pressure.

Stella started by explaining what body image actually means and what self-compassion is. She handed out a bunch of worksheets for us to use, which felt like homework until I started looking through. There are a lot of hard questions in them, but they're all really interesting!

I liked how she didn't just talk *at* us—she started by sharing a story that was really similar to the stories Miss Adler read to us the other day.

She told us this story about a teenager named Emily that she knew—it was obvious she was talking about herself, but I guess it's easier to tell it like a story. Anyway, she said that Emily was smart and talented with a passion for painting and a lot of big dreams. But she hated how she looked. She had always been a little self-conscious about her appearance and she compared herself to the girls on social media, feeling like she never quite measured up. She felt like she had a voice inside of her whispering mean words in her ear, telling her she was too big, too ugly and unworthy of love and acceptance.

But one day, she stumbled upon a self-help book that focused on self-compassion by this big researcher, Kristen Neff, who had discovered it. Self-compassion is this idea of treating yourself with the same kindness and understanding you would offer to a friend in times of need. Emily decided to give the author's advice a try. Stella explained that Emily started by writing in a journal every evening, jotting down her thoughts and feelings. Instead of criticizing herself, she tried to approach her struggles with a sense of understanding and empathy.

Stella explained that Emily realized that these thoughts were not her fault—she was seeing so many unrealistic standards on social media. She started being able to remind herself of her unique qualities and the things she appreciated about herself, not just seeing her flaws.

Stella explained that as Emily continued to do this stuff, she noticed a shift within herself. Her confidence grew, she started to feel more comfortable in her own skin. She realized that true beauty came from self-acceptance, not from conforming to society's unrealistic ideals.

Emily finally decided to share her journey with her closest friends. To her surprise, they too had their own battles with self-image and were inspired by her courage. They formed a support group where they could openly discuss their struggles and practice self-compassion together. Over time, Emily's story spread throughout her community, inspiring others to embrace self-compassion.

She realized that her journey was not just her own but a source of strength for many. Stella let us know that after a few years went by Emily still was continuing to pursue her passion for painting and it even began to reflect the beauty she saw in herself and others, celebrating diversity and the uniqueness of each person. It was really inspiring to hear that she not only felt better about herself but also helped other people!

It felt sort of corny to be so into a story that a teacher (or whatever she is!) was telling us, but the whole class was totally into it. No one made any jokes or passed any notes or anything. We all just sat and listened.

After that, Stella had to close our eyes and think of a time when we felt really upset with ourselves, maybe about our body, schoolwork, or sports. Then she walked us through a "loving kindness meditation", which felt really silly at first, She asked us to place our hand on our heart and say to ourselves, "It's okay to feel this way. I'm doing the best I can. I'm worthy of love and kindness." Saying that out loud in class felt so lame! There were lots of giggles in the classroom because it was so weird, but something about it also felt comforting. Miss Adler turned the lights off to get us to fully tune in and stop giggling, and that seemed to help. There were actually even a few sniffles around the room too... I'm not sure if it was because there supposedly is a bug going around school or if maybe some just felt it a little more than us others. I definitely had to blink back a couple tears.

We got to answer some questions after, and Lilly was the first to speak. She said she had been struggling with comparing herself to other girls, especially when it came to her skin and body, and she always felt like she wasn't good enough. Emma, surprisingly, shared too. She talked about how she feels so much pressure to be good at basketball and to look a certain way to keep up with everyone's expectations, but that sometimes she just wants to eat a burger without worrying about how it might affect her body or her performance.

I was nervous to share, but after hearing them, I felt a little braver. I actually talked about the mirror I found in the attic and how it made me start to see myself in a different way. I told them about the sticky note and how I've started writing kind things to myself. Stella smiled and said that was a perfect example of practicing self-compassion.

She told us three important pieces to practicing self-compassion. They were

1. mindfulness, which means noticing what we're feeling without getting overwhelmed by it
2. self-kindness, which is speaking to ourselves with gentle words, just like how we would talk to a friend, and finally,
3. common humanity, which sounds complicated but just means remembering that everyone makes mistakes, and nobody is perfect. We're all in this together.

Before she left, Stella reminded us that this stuff takes time to cultivate and others may have an easier time than others practicing self-compassion in their every day lives, but it will help if we give it a try.

After the workshop, I wasn't sure if everything would change overnight, but now sitting here on the ground in my room I sort of do feel hopeful that I could start being a little kinder to myself. Lilly, Emma, and I promised to remind each other to practice self-compassion whenever we start being too hard on ourselves.

I'm not sure if Miss Adler wants us to put our worksheet answers in our journals, but I'm going to stick mine in here anyway. I hope you don't mind!

Beyond the Mirror Exercise

The Mirror Exercise helps us build a positive relationship with our reflection. It reminds us to be kind to ourselves, which helps grow self-compassion and encourages us to see ourselves in a more positive light.

Stand in Front of the Mirror: Find a mirror and stand in front of it. Take a moment to look at yourself. Remember, your reflection is your friend. Instead of seeing a mirror as something to judge and be critical, see it as a space where you can say kind things to yourself. Take a moment to think about who you are beyond how you look. Complete these two statements:

- **I am...** (kind, creative, funny, determined, strong, a good friend, etc.)
- **I can...** (be brave, try new things, solve problems, support my friends, stand up for myself, etc.)

I am thoughtful and I do try to help others. I am creative, and I think I might be a good writer.
I can help others when I show up and volunteer. I

can be a good friend even when I'm feeling jealous or comparing myself to them.

Seeing the Power in Yourself: Take a deep breath and look at yourself, recognizing your strength and uniqueness. Say your affirmations out loud while looking at yourself. You can use one from your list or choose one from below:

- "I am worthy of love and kindness."
- "I can face challenges and keep going."
- "I am strong, inside and out."
- "I can be proud of myself for trying new things."

Notice how you feel after saying these affirmations. Does it feel different than what you usually tell yourself?

I tried "I am strong, inside and out." After I said it a few times while looking in the mirror (the one I found in the attic!), I really did feel like I was stronger, just from saying it. I didn't instantly sprout big muscles or anything, but I felt much better than when I look in the mirror usually, and just find the things that I hate.

Reflection & Daily Practice: After completing the exercise, take a moment to reflect:

How did saying these affirmations make you feel?

Powerful!

Which affirmation felt the most powerful?

I like feeling strong.

How can you remind yourself of these affirmations daily?

My sticky note on the mirror!

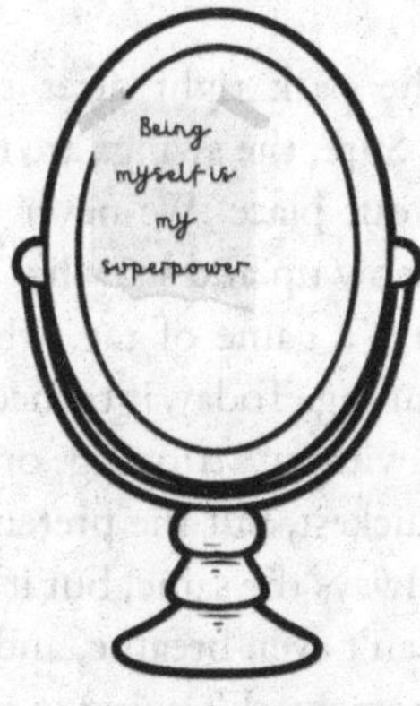

October 1

Dear Diary,

Today I barely had time to catch my breath. School was okay —nothing too exciting, just the usual classes, the annoying pop quiz in history (seriously, who needs to know all those dates?), and the random fire drill that totally threw off my groove. But it didn't matter because after school, I was hanging out with Lilly and Emma, and that's always the best part of my day, especially when it's just hanging out, no pressure about tryouts or other school stuff.

We met up at the park right after school. It's been our hangout spot forever. Sure, the swings are rusty, and the slide's a little bumpy, but it's our place. We never need a plan for these afternoons—we just show up and see what happens. Lilly almost always suggests we play a game of tag, which may be the only time I actually like running. Today, it turned into a game of "who can run the fastest without tripping on the uneven grass." Emma's always the quickest, but she pretends to be "out" just to give us a chance. It's always the same, but it's still fun. We end up laughing so hard we can't even breathe, and I forget about every-thing—like how my homework's going to pile up and how I was supposed to study for that quiz. I sort of lied before—it wasn't really a pop quiz, we knew it was coming, I had just forgotten. I need to write things down better, I guess.

Anyway, after a while, we gave up on tag and decided to sit on the swings. We always end up talking about weird stuff. Today, we ended up chatting about this dream Lilly had last night, where she was running through a giant maze made of jellybeans (I mean, what even is that?). She told us she was trying to find a way out but kept getting distracted by eating the jellybeans, and Emma and I couldn't stop laughing. Like, why would you want to eat jellybeans while you're running for your life in a maze? It just makes no sense, but it was hilarious.

We stayed out until the sun started to set, and the sky was this soft pinkish-purple color. I didn't want to go home, but Lilly's mom called her, and that was our signal that it was time to head back. As we walked home together, we all kept talking about the most random things—like, who we think would survive the longest in a zombie apocalypse (spoiler: Lilly thinks she'd be the last one standing because she's "super stealthy" when she sneaks snacks) and who's the cutest guy in our grade (I'm still convinced it's Kyle from math class, even though Emma totally disagrees).

Before we split up, we promised to meet again tomorrow at the same spot. I'm glad we still have this, even if it sometimes feels like when we're at school, we're growing apart little by little.

Goodnight, Diary. I'm already looking forward to tomorrow. I just hope it doesn't rain.

October 2

Dear Diary,

I was in such a good mood after hanging out with Lilly and Emma yesterday, but of course, my family had to ruin it.

It started at dinner. Mom made spaghetti, which is usually my favorite, but Jake was being extra annoying. He kept making weird noises while chewing, and when I told him to stop, he smirked and did it louder. I tried to ignore him, but then Dad jumped in with one of his dad jokes. "Why did the tomato turn red? Because it saw the spaghetti sauce!"

I swear, he has an endless supply of those. Normally, I'd just roll my eyes and move on, or maybe even laugh, but I was already irritated, so I snapped, "Can we just eat without a comedy show for once?"

Mom gave me the look—the one that says, "You better watch your tone," but I was too annoyed to care. Then Jake, being the little menace he is, went, "Whoa, someone's in a mood." That's when I lost it.

I told him to shut up, and then, of course, Mom got mad at *me*. "You don't speak to your brother like that," she said, as if he wasn't the one provoking me. I tried to argue that he was being annoying on purpose, but Dad just shook his head and muttered something about "teenage hormones." That made me even angrier.

"Maybe I wouldn't be in a mood if everyone in this house took me seriously for once!" I blurted out before storming to my room.

And now here I am, still fuming. It's not even about Jake, really. It's just—why does it always feel like I'm the bad guy for reacting? He gets to be annoying, Dad gets to joke about everything, and I'm the one who's "moody." It's so unfair.

Ugh. I don't even know why I'm letting it get to me. And now all I can think about is how stupid I must've looked storming off like that.

Maybe I need a mantra or something to remind myself that it's okay to have these feelings. I'll think about it after I cool down. I hate feeling this way.

I'm so frustrated! I don't like when I'm like this.

Maybe there's a worksheet for this from Stella. I'll check the folder.

Treat Yourself As You Would A Friend Exercise

Ever wonder what would happen if you treated yourself like your own best friend? It can be helpful, especially when you're having a tough day!

Imagine one of your best friends is having a really hard time or feeling super bad about themselves. How would you help them?

- What would you say to make them feel better?
- What would you do for them?
- How would your voice sound when you're talking to them?

Write down your answers below:

I would tell them they are beautiful just the way they are. I'd remind them of all the amazing things they've done, and that one bad day doesn't define them. I would give them a hug and spend time with them doing something they enjoy, like watching their favorite show or going for a walk. I'd say 'You are enough just as you are. It's okay to feel down sometimes, but remember, you've got so much inside you. You'll get through this.' I'd speak gently, with a warm and comforting tone, so they feel heard and cared for.

Now think about a time when *you* were feeling upset or struggling. How did you talk to yourself?

- What did you say to yourself?
- What did you do?
- What tone of voice did you use in your head?

Write down your answers below:

When I am upset, I usually tell myself I wasn't good enough. I focus on all the things I thought were wrong with me or that I didn't do well enough. I know I'm my own worst critic. In my head, I keep hearing things like, "You're not good enough, Grace. Why can't you just get it together? Why can't you be like everyone else?" And I don't want to get out of the bad mood. I don't want to do anything that might make me feel better. I just stay in my head, feeling stuck and unsure of how to move forward. My voice sounds harsh and disappointed, like I am letting myself down. It makes me feel worse.

Look at your answers. Are they different?

- If they are, why do you think you treat yourself differently than you treat your friends?
- What things make it harder to be kind to yourself?

Yes, they're definitely different. I'm so much kinder to my friends than I am to myself. I give them encouragement, support, and comfort, but I don't do the same for myself. I think maybe it's because I hold myself to higher standards, and I don't want to disappoint anyone. But I need the same love and support as anyone else, and I guess it's okay to be imperfect. Sometimes I feel like I have to have everything figured out or be perfect to deserve kindness. I compare myself to others a lot.

Imagine if you spoke to yourself the same way you'd speak to a friend when they're feeling down. How do you think that would feel? How might it help you?

I think it would feel so much better. I wouldn't feel so alone in my struggles. I'd be more compassionate toward myself, and that might help me feel more capable of handling challenges. It would help me feel less critical and more motivated to take care of myself. If I can be my own friend, maybe I'll be able to work through things more easily. I can imagine how much more peaceful it might feel. I guess I deserve the same kindness I would give to others.

October 6

Today was our class field trip to Wild Ridge Adventure Park, and I am still wired! Not just from the zip line (which was terrifying and awesome at the same time), but from how the whole day felt —like a mix of fun and nerves and a tiny bit of bravery.

At first, I wasn't sure how it would go. The second we got off the bus, all I could think about was how ridiculous I was going to look in a harness. Once I had it on, I kept tugging at the straps, convinced they made me look weird, and of course, Lilly and Emma were already having the time of their lives, not over-thinking a thing. I wish I could be that relaxed!

When we got to the zip line, my stomach basically flipped upside down. Everyone else clipped in like it was no big deal, but my brain was full of *what-ifs*. What if I chickened out? What if I screamed too loud? What if I looked dumb?

But Lilly and Emma weren't letting me back out. "You *have* to try it," Emma said, already halfway in the air. "It's basically flying."

And somehow, I did it. The second I stepped off the plat-form, all the noise in my head disappeared. It was just me, the wind, and this crazy rush of freedom. I *did* scream—but so did everyone else. And when I landed, Lilly and Emma cheered like I'd won a gold medal.

I won't lie—there were still moments where I caught myself overthinking, comparing, worrying about how I looked, especially my hair right after the zip line. Yikes. But I also laughed. A lot.

October 8

Dear Diary,

Guess what? Stella was back in Miss Adler's class today, and it was the best surprise ever! She has this way of making everything she says sound like it's the most important thing in the world. Today, she talked about self-compassion mantras and affirmations. Stella said these little statements are like reminders to be kind to ourselves. She called them "positive seeds" we can plant in our minds, so when tough times come, we can draw strength from them. It made me think of the sticky note I found on the mirror, and the new one I wrote up after I did her Mirror exercise the first day she was here talking to us.

She even shared some examples:

- *Like everyone, I have both strengths and weaknesses.*
- *I believe in my ability to get through tough times.*
- *My body is a miracle.*
- *My body radiates beautiful kindness.*
- *I give my body what it needs.*
- *I am thankful for my body's strength.*
- *I am grateful for my legs that help me walk to school every day.*

The whole time, I couldn't help but think, "Can I really

believe these things about myself?" A big part of me wanted to roll my eyes, but a tiny part of me whispered, "What if it actually works?"

We also had to write our own affirmations, and I decided to give it a shot. Mine were:

- *My body allows me to walk to school every day.*
- *I give my body the food that it needs to grow.*

Okay, they're simple, but saying them felt... nice? Kind of like giving myself a tiny high-five.

Then Stella said something that really stuck: She said that you can apply affirmations to anything in your life. They're not just about your body—they're about reminding yourself that you're enough in every part of your life. That hit me hard. Like, maybe I've been focusing too much on what I'm *not* instead of celebrating what I *am*. Maybe I've been so focused on my body and all the athletic stuff like tryouts and running, but ignoring the rest of me. So, I added another affirmation:

- *I am thankful that I have the creativity to write my own story.*

Stella said it's important to say these affirmations regularly, like brushing your teeth. Which is just what Miss Adler told us about saying nice things to ourselves! It might feel awkward at first, but over time, she swears that it helps you believe them. I don't know about that, but I'm going to start looking in the mirror when I'm brushing my teeth and read my sticky note and see what happens.

Goodnight, Diary. Here's hoping these "positive seeds" start to grow.

October 10

Dear Diary,

This week was a short week at school because there was a teacher in-service day today, and I'm so glad I didn't just waste it sitting around at home. At first, I thought I might just relax and catch up on some TV shows or scroll through my phone, but then Lilly and Emma texted asking if I wanted to go to the mall with them.

Honestly, I wasn't sure at first. I've started to feel a little weird shopping with them. Back to school shopping was so stressful. I mean, they're always so confident, trying on clothes and picking out things that look great on them. I used to love doing the whole fashion show in the change room thing, but in the last year, not so much. But, I went anyway. We ended up spending hours at the mall, just browsing, trying on silly hats and really bright makeup, and getting ice cream. It was nice to not worry about anything for once—no school stress, no overthinking how I look, just us hanging out.

At one point after lunch, they wanted to start trying on clothes, so I went along with it even though I was sure it would be a disaster. But I actually found a cute sweater that I really liked, and I was surprised at how good I felt wearing it. Lilly even said the color—kind of a dark purple—looked amazing on me. She's such a good hype girl! I don't know what I would do without her. When I was trying stuff on, I realized that I wasn't even comparing myself to her or Emma, I was just looking in the mirror at how things looked on me. And the fact that things looked great on them didn't change how I looked—it just means that my friends look great in clothes, not that I automatically look worse. Does that make sense? Maybe the positive seed stuff Stella was talking about really works!

October 14

Dear Diary,

Today started out as any other day, but then... everything kind of fell apart.

We had gym class, and I decided to push myself to wear a sleeveless shirt for the first time in *forever*. My heart was pounding as I left the locker room. At first, no one seemed to notice, which was a relief.

But then Jenny—the queen of snarky comments—walked up with her little crew. She stared at my arms and said loud enough for everyone to hear, "Oh wow, Grace. You're really bold showing that off." And then she even poked my arm! What the heck!

My cheeks burned. I tried to laugh it off, but it felt like everyone was staring. Lilly shot me a sympathetic look, but I was frozen. I could feel the old, familiar urge to shrink back, to hide.

At lunch, the drama continued. I sat down with Emma and Lilly, trying to pretend I didn't care. But then I overheard Jenny at the next table whispering to her friends about how bad I am in gym class. She wasn't even subtle about it! I felt my throat tighten, and for a second, I wanted to run to the bathroom and change back into something that covered me up.

But then Lilly did something amazing. She stood up, walked right over to Jenny, and said, "Do you ever get tired of putting people down?" The whole table went silent. I was stunned. Jenny didn't respond. She smirked, but she didn't have a witty come-back or anything.

After that, Lilly and Emma spent the rest of lunch hyping me up. Emma even said she was impressed by how I held it together and how she would have totally freaked out. That hit me hard because Emma always seems like she has it all figured out. But I guess I only ever see Emma getting praised, I don't think I've ever heard someone make fun of her.

By the end of the day, I was exhausted. I keep thinking about how much easier it would be to just go back to hiding. But then I remember what Miss Adler said about being true to yourself. It's not supposed to be easy.

I learned something today, Diary: authenticity is hard. It's messy and scary and sometimes embarrassing. But it's also power-ful. Jenny's words stung, but they didn't break me. I didn't change—my clothes or my attitude. I just stayed me.

That feels like a win.

October 17

Dear Diary,

Last night, I was scrolling through Instagram, and guess what popped up on my feed? A picture of Jenny and her friends from gym class. They were all looking flawless in matching outfits, and captioned it "Squad Goals." For a second, I felt that old pang of jealousy creeping in. I mean, they looked so perfect. But then I started thinking: How much of that is real? And why do I care so much anyway?

It made me think about a talk Miss Adler gave us earlier this week, about how social media only shows one side of the story—the polished, edited side. And honestly, when I see Jenny in real life, she's not as confident as she seems online—or quite as glowy. Plus, she's always putting others down, like she's trying to distract from something she doesn't want people to notice about her.

Then today, something even weirder happened. My mom came into my room with an old photo album she found in the attic. She sat down on my bed and started flipping through pictures of herself from when she was my age.

"Look at this," she said, pointing to a picture of her wearing bright purple overalls and a giant scrunchie. "I thought I looked ridiculous back then. But now, I see a girl who was just trying to figure herself out."

I laughed because, yeah, the outfit was pretty wild. But then she said something that made me stop.

"I spent so much time worrying about what other people thought of me, Grace. If I could go back, I'd tell myself to just *be*. To stop hiding and let people see the real me."

That hit me hard. It's like Mom and Miss Adler were secretly teaming up to send me the same message: authenticity over conformity.

I gathered up my courage and asked her about the mirror I found. I hadn't mentioned it before, for some reason, but after she shared that, I wanted to know why she had it. I always think of her as being so confident, it's hard to believe she ever struggled.

"Your grandma gave me that mirror with the sticky note on it when I was around your age," she said, and she got this big smile on her face. "I forgot all about it! I can't believe it was still up there in the attic after all these years. I guess maybe that reminder to be ourselves was for both of us." Then she just looked at me and told me I'm growing into someone she's really proud of. And then we both got a little teary.

So here I am, Diary, trying to figure out what being "authentic" even means for me. I think it means not getting sucked into comparing myself to Jenny's Instagram or worrying about whether my clothes are trendy enough. Maybe it also means forgiving myself when I feel insecure.

Tomorrow, I'm going to try something new. No leggings, no long sleeves—just me. It's scary, but if my mom could rock purple overalls, I can at least try to be a little braver too.

Learning Social Media Literacy

MEDIA REALITY CHECK

It's important to keep in mind that social media isn't always real life. It's normally a person's highlight reel, sharing only the things that they want everyone to see. But sometimes, that can make us feel like we don't quite measure up, or we're not doing enough, or we start to feel bad that we don't look a certain way. Rather than letting those types of posts get us down, we can simply notice the feeling—and then come back to our real life, and think of what would make our IRL highlight reel!

Your Turn: Think of a post that made you feel bad or like you had to "measure up." What was it?

Seeing a post of Jenny with all of her friends looking super glamorous and like they were having the best time ever on the weekend while I was home alone.

What's one *real* thing about your life that makes you proud or brings you joy—even if it doesn't get posted?

> *I guess if I look back to that weekend, I actually did exactly what I wanted to do: I stayed home and watched movies with mom. I only felt bad about it afterwards when I saw what other people were posting, but in the moment, it brought me a lot of joy!*

FEEL-GOOD FEED AUDIT

If you spend a lot of time on social media, your feed can really impact how you feel. While getting off of social media or limiting your time online is one way to help control those feelings, you can also start to feel more positive by following content that makes you feel inspired and proud of who you are... And you can mute or unfollow accounts that don't make you feel as good.

What's one kind of post or account that lifts you up?

> *I do like goofy dance videos, since I like to try to follow along and learn the steps, even if I don't record myself doing the dances!*

What's something you can do when a post makes you feel left out, not good enough, or stuck in comparison?

> *I can mute or unfollow the people—but I should also try to notice why it makes me feel that way, and ask if there's anything I can be doing to change that. Like if I'm jealous that Jenny is all glammed up with*

her friends, could I do an at-home mani/pedi with Anna?

SELF-COMPASSION CHECK

Remember: The goal should always be to practice self-kindness instead of comparison.

Write one kind reminder you'll tell yourself next time a post messes with your confidence. (Examples: "I'm more than what I post." / "I don't need to look like her to be enough.")

I don't need to be like anyone else, I can just be me!

<h1 style="text-align:center">October 21</h1>

❧

Dear Diary,

Today, I've been thinking a lot about something Miss Adler said in class about authenticity over conformity. At first, I didn't really get what she meant, but the more I think about it, the more it makes sense. She said, "It's more important to be true to your own values and principles, even if they're different from what everyone else is doing."

It's so easy to feel like I need to fit in all the time—whether it's wearing certain clothes, acting a certain way, or even pretending I'm okay with things that I'm not. It feels like everyone else has it all figured out, and I'm just trying to keep up.

But thinking about what she said, I'm starting to realize how often I've tried to go along with things just to avoid standing out. Like in gym class—I was wearing leggings and long sleeves not because I wanted to, but because I felt like I had to hide parts of myself, like those weird marks I get on my legs and stomach when I've been sitting for a while. I hate how they look. When I tried to change it up with a sleeveless shirt, Jenny did make a mean comment, and that made me feel like I didn't fit in even more. But at the same time, I felt almost good that I was doing something for myself instead of trying to hide. And the fact that she noticed says more about her, right?

Plus, I look at Lilly, who has the same marks on her body as me, and she doesn't care if anyone sees them. She's so confident just being herself, and it's made me think: Why do I care so much about what other people think?

Even Anna, who I haven't seen in real life for a while, with everything she's going through, doesn't try to pretend she's someone she's not. She's silly and bold and so unapologetically herself. She doesn't care if people think her TikTok dances are goofy—she does them because they make her happy. It's inspiring to see someone who's dealing with so much still choose to be true to herself, no matter what.

I guess what I'm trying to say is that I don't want to keep pretending anymore. I don't want to wear clothes that don't feel like me or act like someone I'm not just to fit in. I don't want to follow along with things that don't align with what feels right in my heart.

Being true to myself sounds scary because it means I'll have to stop hiding. But it also feels freeing. Like maybe, if I stop trying so hard to conform, I'll finally figure out who I really am.

So here's my goal for the week: Try to focus more on *authenticity*—on doing what feels right for me, not what I think everyone else wants me to do. It's going to be hard, but I think it's worth it.

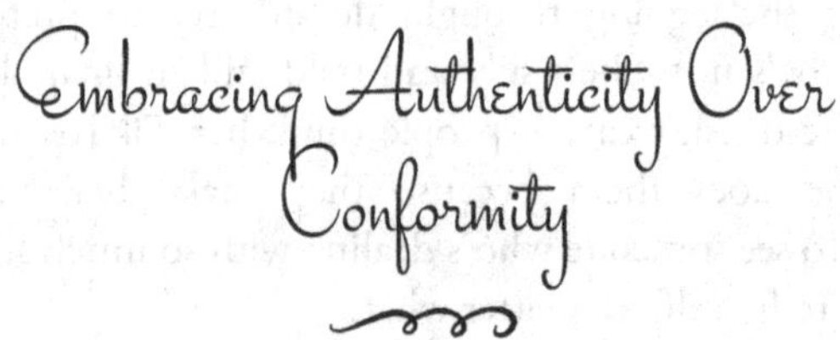

Embracing Authenticity Over Conformity

It can be tempting to follow what everyone else is doing, especially if you feel like you need to fit in. But staying true to who you are—your values, your interests, and what feels right in your heart—is what makes you *really* powerful.

You don't have to do something just because everyone else is doing it. If it doesn't feel right to you, you can make a different choice.

Being yourself means standing by what you believe in. Your opinions, values, and dreams matter, even if they're different from others.

Your uniqueness is your strength. Imagine if superheroes all had the same powers—how boring would that be? The world needs you to be *you!*

Being yourself is your superpower. You don't have to change to fit in. The people who truly matter will appreciate you for who you are.

STEP 1: WHAT MAKES YOU, YOU?

Write down three things that make you unique. These can be your interests, values, or things you care about that may be different from what others think or do.

1. I guess I love writing, but I'm not sure if I'm good enough to share it with others.

2. I don't always feel like I fit in when it comes to what others value or care about. Sometimes, I feel like I'm too different.

3. I care about being a good person and treating people well, but sometimes I wonder if that's enough in a world where people care more about fitting in than being kind.

STEP 2: STAND BY YOUR VALUES

Think of a time when you felt pressured to do something because others were doing it, but it didn't feel right to you. How did it make you feel?How would you handle that situation differently now, knowing it's okay to stay true to yourself?

There was this time when everyone was posting about a new trend on social media, and I felt this pressure to join in, even though I didn't really care about it. I just wanted to be part of the conversation, but I felt awkward and fake doing it.

I think if that happened again, I'd remind myself that it's okay not to be part of everything. I don't have to be like everyone else to be okay. It's okay to just be me, even if I'm not exactly like my friends.

STEP 3: PRACTICE BEING AUTHENTIC

Write down one way you can stay true to yourself in the next week, even if it means doing something differently than your friends. (*Example: "If my friends are talking about a trend I don't like, I'll say it's not my thing but still respect their opinion."*)

Next week, if something comes up that doesn't feel right to me, I'll try saying "I'm not sure about that," even if it's a little uncomfortable. I want to start being more honest about who I am, even if I'm still figuring it out.

STEP 4: CREATE YOUR OWN MANTRA

Think of a phrase or statement that will remind you to stay true to yourself. This will help you when you feel pressured to conform to what others are doing. (*Example: "I trust my own path," or "I am proud of who I am."*)

I'm enough just as I am.

October 24

Dear Diary,

Halloween is supposed to be fun, right? Everyone's excited about their costumes, planning out what they're going to be, but for some reason, it just feels like too much pressure this year. I was trying to think of how to bring the 'new me' to a costume, but it all feels like too much. I've been sitting here for hours, scrolling through ideas, and I just can't find anything I actually like. It's like all these costumes are either too cheesy or too complicated. And it doesn't help when people around me act like Halloween is the one time a year you have to be someone else to have fun.

I'm honestly just tired of trying to fit into this box of what people think Halloween should be. I hate feeling like I'm supposed to love dressing up, but deep down, it just doesn't feel like me. I don't know why, but I always feel like I'm not doing it right. Everyone else seems to have it figured out, and here I am—stressed about what to wear, unsure of what I even *want* to be.

It's frustrating because I love the idea of celebrating the season—the pumpkins, the autumn air, the spooky vibes—but when it comes to the costume part, I just feel lost. I want to have fun, but right now, it feels like a whole lot of pressure to be someone I'm not. Maybe I'll just skip the costume this year, or maybe I'll just wear something simple and not overthink it. Who knows? But right now, I'm feeling really off about it all. Maybe I should try the self-compassion worksheet that Stella gave us.

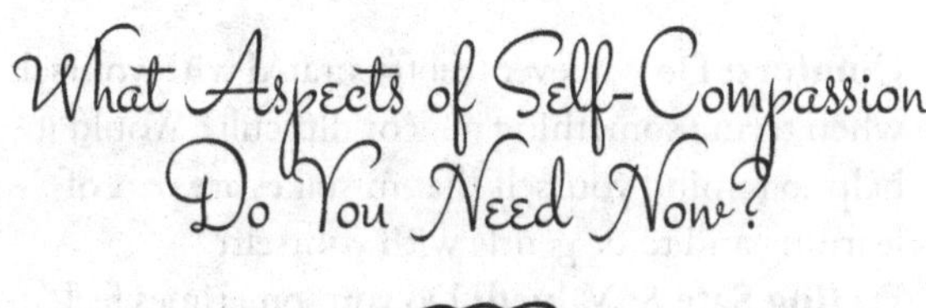

Self-compassion is more than just being kind to yourself—it has different aspects that help us feel safe, supported, and motivated. Below are six ways you can practice self-compassion. Read through them and think about which one you might need most right now:

Comforting – Supporting yourself like you would a friend when you're feeling down. *Example: "I am gentle with myself when I make mistakes."*

Soothing – Helping yourself feel calm and relaxed, especially when things feel stressful. *Example: "I can take deep breaths and remind myself that I am okay."*

Validating – Recognizing and accepting your own feelings as real and important. *Example: "I am allowed to feel what I feel, and my emotions matter."*

Protecting – Setting boundaries and standing up for yourself when needed. *Example: "I can say no to things that make me uncomfortable or unsafe."*

Providing – Giving yourself what you truly need, whether it's rest, support, or fun. *Example: "I can take breaks when I need them, and that's okay."*

Motivating – Encouraging yourself like a good coach—with kindness instead of criticism. *Example: "I am capable, and I can keep going even when things feel hard."*

Take a moment to think about how you treat yourself. Self-compassion means being kind to yourself, just like you would be to a close friend. Read the questions below and reflect on what you might need most right now:

- **Comfort:** Do you ever feel frustrated with yourself when trying something new or difficult? Would it help to remind yourself that mistakes are part of learning and to be gentle with yourself?
- **Feeling Safe & Valued:** Do you sometimes feel alone in your feelings? Would it help to remind yourself that your emotions are real and that it's okay to feel what you feel?
- **Taking Care of Your Needs:** Do you listen to what your body and mind need? Would you like to get better at knowing when to rest, take breaks, or ask for help?
- **Encouraging Yourself:** When things get hard, do you motivate yourself with kindness or criticism? Would it help to talk to yourself like a supportive coach instead of being too hard on yourself?

Think about which area feels most important for you right now. If you want, write down one kind thing you can say to yourself based on what you need. Self-compassion is a skill—you can practice it just like anything else! **Write your answers below:**

Right now, I think I need the most help with Comforting and Validating. I've been feeling a little overwhelmed lately with school and trying to figure out who I am, and I sometimes get frustrated with myself for not being perfect. I tend to be really hard on myself, especially when things don't go the way I want them to.

Comforting: Lately, I've been feeling frustrated with myself, especially when I mess up or don't get things right the first time. I always think I should be able to figure everything out quickly, and when I don't, it feels like I'm failing. Maybe it would help if I reminded myself that it's okay to make mistakes. I need to be kinder to myself and treat myself like I would treat a friend, not like I'm constantly letting myself down.

Soothing: There are definitely times when I feel so stressed, especially with everything going on at school. When I feel overwhelmed, I just want to hide away and hope everything gets better, but I don't always take the time to relax. Maybe if I focused on taking deep breaths or just letting go of the tension in my body, it would help me feel a bit better.

Validating: Sometimes I feel like my feelings don't matter or that I'm being too emotional. It's hard when I get upset or anxious about things and feel like no one else feels the same way—like how nervous I am about trying out for a team. But I think I need to remind myself that it's okay to feel how I feel. My emotions are valid, and they're part of who I am. I don't need to apologize for feeling them.

Protecting: This one's tough for me. I tend to say yes to things, even if I'm not really okay with them, because I don't want to let people down. I think I need to work on setting boundaries more—saying no when I feel like I need to, whether it's because I'm too busy or something just doesn't feel right. It's okay to protect myself from situations that don't feel good.

Providing: I definitely need to be better about listening to myself when I'm tired. Sometimes I push myself too hard, trying to do everything perfectly. I need to remember that it's okay to take a break when I need one, and that I deserve rest and time to recharge. I can't be on all the time.

Motivating: When things get tough, I can be really critical of myself. It's like I expect myself to always be perfect, and if I'm not, then I think I've failed. I want to try being more encouraging to myself, like a coach would be. I'm capable of more than I think, and I can keep going even when it's hard.

Kind Thing I Can Say to Myself: I am doing the best I can, and that's enough. It's okay not to have everything figured out. I'm learning and growing, and I don't need to be perfect. Maybe next year will be different, but for now, I'm just going to give myself permission to feel frustrated about it. Not every moment has to be perfect.

Dear Diary

Today gave me a lot to think about. I spent the afternoon hanging out with Anna: I wasn't volunteering, she just messaged me and asked if I wanted to come to the hospital and hang out with her. I asked Mom and she said yes, like it was no big deal, but I could tell she was happy that I made a friend through volunteering. While I was there, we talked about all kinds of things—mostly about our lives and what we've been learning recently. Anna's so open and real, and it's been really nice to connect with someone who's going through some tough stuff but still manages to be so genuine.

We got into a conversation about Stella and the stuff she's taught our class, all the self-compassion stuff and about how we treat ourselves. Anna was curious about the "mirror activity" Miss Adler had us try, so I told her about how it's been helping me notice the little things I like about myself. Honestly, I think Anna found it kind of silly at first, but as we kept talking, I could tell it made sense to her in a way too. She mentioned how she sometimes gets caught up in feeling like she has to be strong all the time, especially with everything she's dealing with. If she starts to think negatively or feel weak, she's afraid that's going to make her sicker.

We talked about how Stella says that being kind to ourselves isn't just about positive thinking—it's about really accepting ourselves as we are, even the messy parts. Anna nodded a lot while I was talking. It's like, we both know we can't just fix everything by looking in a mirror or saying a few affirmations, but there's something comforting about knowing that we're allowed to be gentle with ourselves while we work through the hard stuff.

Anna also told me how, sometimes, when things get really rough, she feels like she has to pretend everything's fine just to make other people in her life feel better. I told her about the things Stella was saying that it's okay to not be okay sometimes, and that it's okay to ask for help. I think we both agreed that being *real* is so much better than pretending.

As we were hanging out, I realized something: I've been feeling a lot of pressure to keep up with everyone else, to look a certain way and act a certain way, but Anna doesn't seem to feel that pressure at all. It's like she's had to move past it because of being sick, but that's actually helped her become a really cool person. So maybe I should focus on trying to be more me, instead of trying to fit in. I don't have to change myself just to fit into other people's boxes, even if I don't always feel strong or confident while being myself.

Now I just need to figure out exactly who 'me' is!

Even if I have a lot more thinking to do, it was such a good conversation, and it made me feel like I'm not alone in this journey. Anna gets it, and she's not afraid to be herself, even when life's not easy. I think I'm starting to believe that I can do the same.

Goodnight, Diary.

November 1

So, what did I do for Halloween? I ended up staying home with Mom. While Dad took Jake trick or treating, we made popcorn, lit a pumpkin-scented candle, and watched some old scary movies while we handed out candy to little kids. I actually liked it at first — it felt cozy and safe, like our own little world. I didn't have to worry about costumes or feeling out of place. It was just us.

But then, there was a knock at the door.

It was Emma and Lilly, dressed up and laughing. They looked so cute — Emma was a vampire and Lilly was a witch, and they had clearly been having the best time trick-or-treating. I smiled and tried to act normal, but inside, this weird, twisty feeling bubbled up. Like... I was missing out. Like maybe I should have gone with them after all. (They invited me, I just said I was busy.)

Emma was like, "Grace! Why didn't you come? We missed you!"

And before I could even answer, Lilly kind of joked, "Yeah, you're such a hermit lately!" She didn't mean it in a mean way, but it stung. More than I wanted to admit.

I mumbled something about not feeling like it, but Mom chimed in with, "We just wanted a quiet night." She meant well, but it made me feel even more childish — like I couldn't handle being out there with everyone else.

The words just slipped out before I could stop them: "You don't get it. None of you do."

There was this super awkward silence. Emma and Lilly tried to laugh it off, but I could tell they were hurt. And Mom looked worried, like she wasn't sure what to say.

After they left, I kind of spiraled. I felt guilty for snapping at them. I felt lame for staying home. I felt mad at myself for not just getting over it and joining in. It was like no matter what I did, I couldn't win.

That's when I remembered one of the self-compassion worksheets Stella had given us. At first, I didn't want to touch it — I was too mad at myself. But eventually, I opened it up and tried the "Self-Compassion Break." It has three parts:

1. **Mindfulness:** "This is a moment of pain."
2. **Common humanity:** "Other people feel this way too. I'm not alone."
3. **Self-kindness:** "May I be kind to myself right now."

Saying those words — even just whispering them in my head — actually helped.

I didn't magically feel better, but it was like... I stopped fighting myself so hard. I realized it's okay that I needed a quiet night. It's okay that I felt a little jealous, a little left out. It's okay to not have it all figured out.

Maybe being kind to myself when things aren't perfect is a different kind of bravery. I'm still not much closer to figuring out who I really am, but I think being someone who recharges in a cozy way at home instead of being out with a bunch of people is part of it. Hm. Maybe these tough moments actually are good ways for me to figure out who I am, and if I like it!

Self-Compassion Break

Think about a situation in your life that feels hard or stressful right now. Maybe it's a tough day at school, a disagreement with a friend, or feeling nervous about something. Take a deep breath and notice how this stress feels in your body. Now, say to yourself:

This is a tough moment.
That's mindfulness—recognizing what's happening without ignoring it. Other ways to say this:
-"This feels really hard right now."
-"I don't like how this feels."
-"This is stress, and that's okay."

Struggles are part of life.
That's common humanity—reminding yourself that you're not alone. Other ways to say this:
-"Everyone has hard days."
-"I'm not the only one who feels this way."
-"It's okay to struggle sometimes."

Now, place your hands over your heart or give yourself a gentle hug—whatever feels most comforting. Take another deep breath.

May I be kind to myself.
Ask yourself: What do I need to hear right now? Choose a phrase that feels right for you:
-"May I give myself the kindness I need."
-"May I accept myself just as I am."
-"May I be patient with myself."
-"May I be strong."
-"May I remember that I am enough."

You can use this anytime you're feeling overwhelmed. Self-compassion isn't about ignoring hard feelings—it's about learning to be there for yourself, just like you would for a friend.

November 4

Dear Diary,

This week everyone is freaking out again about basketball tryouts, this time for the local basketball winter travel team. Of course, Emma is trying out, and Lilly is too. I'm honestly feeling a little overwhelmed. Everyone around me seems so excited about it, but I can't shake this nagging feeling inside. All of Miss Adler's talk about self-expression and authenticity really got me thinking—do I actually *want* to play basketball, or am I just doing it because it's what I've always done? What if I've been pushing myself into things just to fit in, instead of because I actually enjoy them?

I've been trying to figure out why I am trying out in the first place if I don't really like it. Or do I not like it because I put so much pressure on myself to want to be the best but I am not built that way? I think a big part of it is not wanting to disappoint Emma and Lilly. After Halloween, I called both of them and apologized for not hanging out with them and explained I was just really feeling like I needed some quiet time, and they both said they understood, but I'm not totally sure they did. Still, we're okay. They weren't mad at me, and things felt back to normal at school. But if I also don't attempt to be on the same team as them, will they take it the wrong way?

So I actually went to watch a game today. The boys were playing. The players on the court were so into it—like they were in their element, and it made me wonder if I've ever really felt that way about basketball. So, I called Anna to talk to her about it, since I figured she might have a different point of view than Emma or Lilly, who just like playing basketball. I knew Anna would be blunt with me, and she didn't disappoint. She said something that really hit me: "You don't need to be good at everything. Just do what makes you feel like *you*." I guess that's true, right? I don't have to keep doing things just to fit in. I can choose what feels right for me. I don't know why it's so hard!

And even knowing I don't want to try out, I'm still unsure. Part of me feels like it's okay to step back if it doesn't feel right. I don't want to keep doing something just to make other people proud or because it's expected of me. I want to do what makes me feel like *me*, whether that's basketball or something else entirely. But I don't want to lose my friends and who they think I am either.

I think I'm going to go to tryouts, but with an open mind. I won't force myself into it if it doesn't feel right. It's scary to think about, but I know that figuring out who I really am means being honest with myself, even if it's not what others expect.

So, here's to trying new things, figuring it out, and, most importantly, staying true to myself.

November 6

Dear Diary,

Sometimes it feels like Miss Adler can read our minds—or is spying on us in the cafeteria. Today in health class when we walked into the room, she had the whiteboard covered in drawings of lunch trays and all sorts of foods, broccoli, cookies, rice, apples, even samosas and spaghetti.

I hadn't eaten much again today because I was feeling weird about what I packed. I packed leftovers from dinner—very spicy and kind of messy—and I wasn't sure if anyone else would be eating something like that. Plus, I don't really like leftovers. But then, just seeing the drawings on the board made me hungry!

Miss Adler started talking about how food isn't "good" or "bad," and how we don't have to earn it. That felt really nice to hear. She also told us that as we're getting older and "developing" (ahem, starting to need bras!) we need to fuel our bodies so they can make these big changes, and it's even more true if we're also playing sports and stuff. I tried not to stare at Emma when she said that. And then Miss Adler even went on to say we should call food by its name like "cookie" instead of "junk food" and that we can enjoy all sorts of flavors and textures. I loved that. Especially because sometimes, I like dipping pickles in hummus and I thought that was just a me thing.

She also talked about how food connects us to family and

memories, and that we each have different foods we eat because of our culture, traditions, or just what's in our cupboards. It made me think of Grandma's bread, the one she only makes on holidays and everyone lines up for a slice.

At the end, she asked us to draw a plate filled with foods we like, not just foods we think we're supposed to like. Mine had mango, rice, cheese cubes, and a brownie. Yum! And you know what? With everyone doing the activity together, I didn't feel weird about it. I could see the other girls getting into it and I noticed Emma nodding along a couple of times and really focusing on her drawing. I hope this means we can all stop watching what each other is doing at lunch and just enjoy our food again. I know it's not that simple, but the talk definitely helped me feel better and more able to make my own choices about food and what makes me feel good!

<h1 style="text-align:center">Creative Outlet Exploration</h1>

Being yourself means finding ways to show the world who you are—through the things you love, the clothes you wear, or the activities that make you happy. Maybe you love drawing, writing, playing music, or putting together outfits that feel *so you.* The more time we spend doing things we love, the happier we feel. Self-expression is all about showing the world what makes you unique!

STEP 1: FIND YOUR CREATIVE OUTLET

Take a moment to reflect on what makes you, *you!* Fill in the blanks below:

What is something you've always loved doing? *(Examples: painting, writing, playing an instrument, dancing, designing outfits, coding, photography, etc.)*

I love doing: I'm not totally sure yet. I've tried a few things, like writing and taking photos, but I'm still figuring it out.

. . .

What is something you'd like to try but haven't yet?

Maybe painting or learning how to play an instrument.

If you had a free day to do whatever you wanted, what would you do?

I would probably take a walk, read a book, and maybe try something new like painting, and of course hang out with Emma, Lilly or Anna.

STEP 2: MAKE TIME FOR YOU

Your Challenge: Set aside 30 minutes this week to do something creative that makes you feel happy and free!

Pick one thing from your list or try something totally new! Some ideas: <u>Paint a picture</u> | Write a short story | Sing your favorite song | Dance to your favorite music | Act out a scene from your favorite movie | Design a video game | Try on a totally new outfit from your closet | Reorganize or rearrange your room

I'm going to invite Lilly over for painting and baking night maybe. Lilly is so good at art that I'm a little nervous doing a painting project with her, but at least I know she'll enjoy it.

STEP 3: EXTRAORDINARY IN THE ORDINARY

Even the little things you do every day can help you express your-self! Here are a few simple ways to celebrate who you are:

- Write one sentence about how your day went.
- Sing a song that makes you smile.
- Wear an outfit that feels comfortable and fun to you.

Remember: The world is a better place when you show what makes you unique. Your creativity, ideas, and passions are *extraordinary!* "No one else is YOU, and that is your superpower."

November 7

Dear Diary,

I decided to invite Lilly over after school to paint with me. She's actually super artistic, and I figured it could be fun to give it a go, even though I'm not great at painting. When I asked her if she wanted to, she said yes right away and muttered something about needing a break from basketball, so I guess it's not just me feeling overwhelmed about tryouts and all the competitiveness going around lately.

We didn't have any painting supplies so Mom took us to the Dollar Store to get some and it was so much fun! We went down the aisles looking for paint and brushes, and I didn't know what I was doing, but Lilly was super into picking bright neon colors. I decided to go with pastel colors, like soft pink and light blue, because they looked calming.

Then, we made a pit stop in the candy aisle (obviously) and picked out all our favorites—gummy worms, chocolate bars, and chips. It felt like we were in the best mood ever by the time we checked out.

Once we got back to my place, we spread out all the paint and got started. Lilly showed me how to mix colors to create different shades of a color, and I was honestly surprised at how fun it was. My painting definitely wasn't perfect, but I didn't really care. It just felt good to paint and not worry about it being "right." I had no idea I'd enjoy it so much, even though I didn't know what I was doing at first.

It was such a fun night. I'm really glad I decided to try something new. I think I might paint again soon. Maybe I'm starting to find something I actually like. I almost brought up not trying out for basketball, but Lilly had seemed so stressed about it when I called her that I didn't want to bring it up. She never seems stressed, so I was a little nervous. Maybe I should have. Maybe we could have had a real conversation about it. Maybe next time.

Dear Diary

Well, I don't even know where to start. Today went completely off the rails. There was a huge fight with Emma over tryouts, and I'm still trying to figure out what just happened.

Here's the thing: Yes, originally we all decided we were going to try out for the basketball team this year. I did once. I didn't really want to then, but I went along with it because everyone else seemed so excited about it, and I didn't want to be the one to back out. I thought maybe I could make it work, maybe surprise myself, or maybe I could even *like* basketball if I just gave it a chance. But the truth is, I hate it. I'm terrible at it.

During the first set of tryouts earlier this year, I felt like everything was going wrong. I couldn't dribble without tripping over my own feet, and when I tried to shoot the ball, it always missed. And I could feel the pressure of everyone's eyes on me, especially Emma's.

But here's the part I don't get. Up until now, Emma has always been so supportive—like, she's always been the one who encouraged me to try new things and told me I could do it. She didn't mind when I didn't make the first team, she just said we'd keep practicing and I'd make the next team. But today? She was different.

The tryouts were being held in the afternoon, so during

recess, we were practicing. After I missed yet another shot, she just snapped. She said I wasn't even trying, that I should be putting in more effort, and that I was just being lazy. I couldn't believe it. Where was this coming from? She's never been like that with me before. It felt like she was expecting me to be great at this, and when I wasn't, she got mad.

I don't know what's changed with her. Maybe it's because she's the star on the team now and she doesn't want me to mess it up? But I've never seen her like this, and it kind of caught me off guard. I mean, yeah, I'm not great at basketball, but I thought she'd be there to support me, not make me feel worse about it.

I couldn't hold it in anymore. I told her I didn't want to keep doing this. I said I was only trying out because everyone else was, and that I didn't actually enjoy basketball, and I emailed the coach to say that I was taking myself off the tryout roster. (He was really nice about it, he didn't even tell me that I wouldn't have made the team anyway!)

But then Emma just totally went off. She said I was ruining the whole thing and that I was being selfish. That I didn't care enough to even try. It was like the Emma I knew had completely disappeared, and in her place was this person who just seemed frustrated and mad at me.

We both got really angry. And I feel like I don't even know her right now. She didn't even want to listen to why I felt the way I did. She just kept telling me I was letting everyone down. So, I snapped back, and I told her maybe I didn't *care* about basketball the way she did. Maybe it wasn't about impressing everyone else, but about finding something I actually enjoy. She said if that was the case, maybe I should find another friend who doesn't force me to do things I hate. She was being sarcastic, but I saw that she was also tearing up as we yelled at each other.

Lilly didn't say anything the whole time, in case you were wondering. She kind of faded into the background and sort of just exited the situation entirely. I don't really blame her, clearly this wasn't about her at all and I wouldn't have wanted to be in the middle of it either.

Anyway, now Emma and I aren't speaking, I think. I don't

know if she's actually mad at me or just upset about the tryouts, but I hate this. I feel like I'm caught in the middle—like I'm disappointing her if I don't want to play, but I'm also pretending to be something I'm not if I keep going with this.

I don't know what to do. I feel like Emma has changed somehow, and I don't know if I should keep pushing through with basketball or just quit and risk losing her. But then again, I can't keep doing something just because everyone else wants me to. I don't even know what I want anymore.

Goodnight, Diary.

November 17

Dear Diary,

It feels like forever since I last wrote, but I don't know where to start. Life has been... a lot. Like, too much all at once. I've thought about picking you up a hundred times, but every time I did, it felt like I didn't even know how to put all the stuff swirling around in my head into words. But here I am. Maybe putting it all down will help.

First off, Emma. Ugh. I still don't know what's going on with her. It's like one day we were laughing so hard we can't breathe, and the next, she's all quiet and distant, like I've done something wrong. I mean, did I? I've replayed every conversation from before tryouts in my head, trying to figure it out, but it's like trying to piece together a puzzle when half the pieces are missing. Being around her used to feel like home, but now it's... weird. And I hate it. Lilly and I are still talking and we're fine, but Emma and I haven't talked in a full week, which is forever for us. I can tell Lilly is upset about the fight but she hasn't brought it up, so I haven't either. I'm sort of hoping it just blows over and the Emma I know comes back.

And ugh. I know we've been told in health class that our bodies will be changing really fast as we get older, but to be honest, Diary, I know it's natural and normal and all of that, but right now, I absolutely hate it. Everything feels *different*. Take my favorite jeans for example. They used to be my go to for everything. But now? They pinch at my waist, like they're mad at me for growing. I spent 10 minutes trying to stretch them out by squatting in my room before school the other day, but they still felt wrong... the gym shorts we have to wear don't sit right on me, and even my favorite never-let-me-down hoodie feels weird. I look in the mirror, and it's like I don't recognize myself anymore. I feel like my body is this alien thing I don't understand, and I just want to crawl out of my own skin.

How can you go from being you to being a complete stranger over one weekend?! So much for figuring out who I am, how am I supposed to do that when everything is changing constantly?

Everyone says it's "just part of growing up," but you know what? Growing up sucks. Sometimes I just wish I could hit rewind and go back to when everything felt easy. Back when Emma and I just were friends and normal. Back when I didn't feel so self-conscious about every little thing.

Everything just feels so *hard* right now. I know I'm supposed to be strong, but honestly? I don't feel strong. I feel like I'm stumbling around, trying to figure out where I fit.

But maybe that's why I'm back here, writing to you. Because even if I feel like a mess, at least here I can be messy. And maybe that's okay.

November 19

Dear Diary,

I swear Miss Adler can read our minds. It's creepy but also kind of amazing. It was one of those gray, drizzly fall mornings where everyone seemed half-asleep, and I was sitting in class trying to focus on anything other than the fact that my jeans were still digging into my stomach. I kept pulling at the waistband, hoping no one would notice. Emma was sitting a few seats away, twirling her pencil, and we haven't talked since our fight. It felt like this huge, invisible bubble of awkwardness was just floating between us, making everything harder. Miss Adler walked in with her usual big smile, carrying a stack of papers that looked way too serious for a usual rainy movie day in class.

She put them on her desk, looked around the room, and said, "Okay, class, I've been hearing some talk on recess duty that we need to address." Yikes.

The room perked up a little. Even Emma stopped twirling her pencil. Then Miss Adler said we needed to talk about body image. I froze. I didn't even want to make eye contact. It was like she'd aimed a spotlight right at me. My stomach flipped. She started the talk by asking us why we think we're so hard on ourselves sometimes.

No one said much at first. A few kids looked down at their

desks. Others fidgeted with their erasers. I just kept doodling random swirls in the margins of my notebook, hoping she wouldn't call on me. But then Miss Adler mentioned Stella's talk from a few weeks ago. She said, "Remember how Stella told us to think about how we speak to ourselves? How we'd never talk to our friends the way we sometimes talk to our own reflection?" I remembered sitting in that class, listening to Stella's story. I felt so seen that day, like she was describing everything I've been too afraid to say out loud. But now, weeks later, it was like I'd forgotten all of it. The old voice in my head, the one that's never happy with how I look or what I do, has taken over again.

Stella was right. We know what we should do to treat ourselves better, but it's easy to know it, and harder to do it.

Miss Adler paused and looked right at us as we all awkwardly fidgeted. "I've been thinking," she said. "Maybe we should have Stella come back for another class. I feel like this is a conversation we need to keep having."

I felt my throat tighten. I wasn't sure if it was relief or nerves, but the idea of hearing from Stella again made something inside me relax—just a little. Maybe hearing her speak again would remind me that I'm not alone in all of this. Even knowing that people like Miss Adler are paying attention to what we're going through and actually care makes me feel a little less lonely.

Miss Adler handed out blank sheets of paper and asked us to write down one kind thing we could say to ourselves today. I stared at mine for what felt like forever. My brain was screaming, Nothing. There's nothing kind to say. But then I remembered something Stella had said: "Start small. Even the tiniest step counts."

So, I wrote the last thing I wrote on one of those worksheets:
I'm trying my best, and that's enough.

It felt weird at first, like the words didn't belong to me. But as I wrote it out, the tightness in my chest started to ease. I think for the first time in a while, I realized that even though these struggles with body image aren't going to magically disappear overnight, I'm not facing them alone. I have Lilly and Anna, I maybe have

Emma, and I know Miss Adler and my mom and dad all are there for me. And I guess I'm learning how to be there for myself too, in a way that feels genuine.

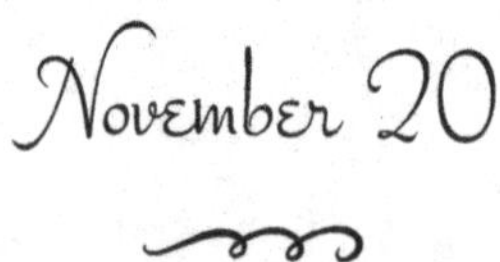

November 20

Dear Diary,

I actually made up with Emma today! Yes, after everything that happened with tryouts, I was so angry, but I think we both realized how silly we were being and we were just being stubborn by not talking. After writing to myself that I was trying my best yesterday, I started thinking: Was I really trying my best when it came to Emma and our friendship? I realized I wasn't. I was just waiting for an apology. Yes, she was wrong, but I should have talked to her much earlier about how I felt about basketball, not just waited until tryouts when I knew she was already really stressed.

So at lunch, I sat down and apologized for not being upfront about how much I was struggling with basketball. She apologized for snapping at me, and we both cried a little and hugged. Lilly cried too and just said that she was so relieved we had made up. I think she was happier than either of us! Emma and I both kind of admitted that we were just feeling a lot of pressure—me from trying to fit in, and her from trying to keep everything together. We all talked for a long time, and I think it helped us realize that it's okay to have different priorities. I might not be a basketball player, and that's okay. I can still be a part of the team in my own way, even if I'm not trying to be the star player like she is.

It felt good to talk it out, and even though things aren't

perfect, I'm glad we've started to understand each other again. Sometimes it feels like things just fall apart, but then you have moments like this that remind you how important it is to be honest with each other and with yourself.

I'm feeling a little more at peace tonight. It's still a work in progress, but I think I'm starting to get there.

<h1 style="text-align:center">November 22</h1>

Dear Diary,

I realized something today. It's been weeks since I've looked in the mirror I found in the attic with the sticky note. Life just got busy—school projects, basketball tryouts...which I didn't make the team, and the chaos with Emma and Lilly. I've just felt so... not like myself. And I just didn't want to even look at myself in that mirror, because when I saw myself in my regular full length closet mirror, I hated what I saw. And that made me scared to look.

I was scared that what it showed me before wouldn't still be there, but I stopped wanting to pick up that little mirror, the mirror that made me feel so good. I was afraid it would confirm what I was afraid of: That I look totally different, and not in a good way.

But today, while helping Mom again, I caught a glimpse of my reflection in the kitchen window. For a second, I thought about how I've been feeling lately—kind of stuck, like I'm just going through the motions. I've been comparing myself to everyone again, and it's exhausting. Mom keeps saying how important it is to give back, but honestly, I've been so wrapped up in my own stuff that I haven't really wanted to help.

That's when it hit me: I needed to look in my special mirror.

So after dinner, I went upstairs, pulled it out from where I had stashed it under my bed, and set it on my desk. It felt a little strange at first, like seeing an old friend you haven't talked to in a while. But then I took a deep breath and just... let myself look.

At first, it was just me. Same awkward feeling creeping in. But then, slowly, the reflection began to shift, just like it had before as I read the sticky note over and over. When I looked again, I saw myself in a good light. I closed my eyes, still thinking "being myself is my superpower." And with my eyes closed, I saw myself surrounded by people—kids my age and younger—laughing, smiling, and helping out at one of Mom's events. I was handing out backpacks to kids, my arms full, my heart light. I looked happy. Confident. Like I had found a way to step out of my own head and focus on something bigger.

I opened my eyes and it felt like the mirror was reminding me of something I'd forgotten: that when I stop focusing so much on the negative parts of myself, I can actually make a difference for others.

I don't know why I'd let myself drift away from that. Mom's been talking a lot lately about how volunteering isn't just about helping others—it's about finding purpose and connecting with the world around you. She also mentioned that when I get to high school, I'll need volunteer hours to graduate. But maybe it's not just about the hours. Maybe this is something I can start doing now, not because I have to, but because it feels right.

So tonight, I told Mom I want to help more. Not just with sorting donations in the living room, but really help—maybe organizing something special for the kids in the wing Anna stays in. She practically lit up when I said it.

I think I'm ready to stop hiding from the mirror and from myself. If that reflection is even a little bit of who I can be, I want to try. It feels like I'm starting to understand that how I see myself isn't just about the mirror—it's about the stories I tell myself, the ones I hear from others, and how they all shape the way I feel. For the first time in a long time, I didn't want to shrink away. I just wanted to wrap my arms around myself, just for a second, and say, *Hey, you're doing okay.* Maybe even more than okay. Today, I felt like giving myself a hug. So I did. I crossed my arms and squeezed, letting myself feel the warmth, the comfort, the reminder that I'm here, I'm trying, and that's enough. And if you're reading this, maybe try it too. Just wrap your arms around yourself, even if it feels silly. Take a deep breath and remind yourself—you are enough, just as you are.

November 24

Dear Diary,

As we've been waiting to talk about body image, I couldn't help but notice how conversations always seemed to circle back to the same topic: bodies, appearances, and who looked like what after summer break. Honestly, I still don't fully get what body image even *is*. Like, what does it really mean to have a "positive body image" or a "negative body image"? Is it just about how I look in the mirror, or is it deeper than that?

I know it can't be just about the number on the scale or how my clothes fit, because there are days when I feel okay about how I look, and other days, it feels like I can't even look at myself without feeling bad, even though nothing has really changed. It's so confusing. Sometimes it feels like I should be confident in my body, but it's hard when I see what everyone else is doing or how they look. I mean, how am I supposed to figure it all out when even the adults seem unsure? And I have noticed it isn't just the girls either; the boys had their own opinions too. Sometimes, it felt like every comment was just another reminder of how much we're all thinking about how we look, even when we're pretending not to.

At lunch, I overheard Jenny and Chloe talking about the latest TikTok trend. They were laughing about some viral dance but also making comments about the influencer who started it—

about how perfect her hair was, how toned her arms looked, how fit she was.

"She's so pretty," Chloe said, almost dreamily. "I wish I looked like that."

Jenny nodded in agreement, scrolling through her phone. "Yeah, same. It's like... how do people even look like that? It's unfair." Even though these are the girls that are always putting others down.

I sat there quietly, my sandwich suddenly feeling heavy in my hands. I knew the influencer they were talking about—her videos were all over my feed too. She was everywhere. And even though I tried to remind myself that social media doesn't show the whole picture, it was hard not to compare myself to her, or to anyone else, really. It's like those perfect images were burned into my brain, and no matter how much I tried to push them out, they always snuck back in.

That afternoon in class, Miss Adler started a discussion that felt like she had been reading my mind. We were talking about media and advertising, but then the conversation shifted to how TV, movies, and social media play a huge role in how we see ourselves.

"Can anyone tell me what they think about the images we see online?" Miss Adler asked, looking around the room. "Do you think they're real? Or are they trying to sell us something?"

A few hands shot up. Lilly was the first to speak. "I think a lot of it's fake. Like, it's not how people really look in real life. They use filters and stuff, right?"

Miss Adler nodded. "Exactly. Filters, editing, makeup—there's a lot of work that goes into creating those images, and we don't always realize it. They set these standards for beauty that aren't realistic for most people."

Another classmate, Jordan, raised his hand. "But if we know it's fake, why do people still care about it so much? Like, if we all know it's not real, why does it matter?"

Miss Adler smiled, clearly pleased with the question. "That's a great point, Jordan. Even though we know it's not real, we still see it all the time. It's like being told over and over again that we need to look a certain way to be accepted or admired. When we see the same images and messages repeated, it can start to feel like those things are true, even when we know better."

As she spoke, I started thinking about all the times I'd compared myself to the girls I saw online. I knew, deep down, that most of what I saw wasn't real. But knowing that didn't stop me from wishing I looked more like them—or at least wondering if people would like me more if I did.

Miss Adler called on me next—I had put my hand up without even thinking about it! "What about you, Grace? What do you think about these media images? Do you think they've impacted the way you see yourself?" I hesitated. Part of me didn't want to answer, but I felt it every day—the pressure to look a certain way, to be pretty enough, fit enough, perfect enough. And I wasn't the only one.

"I guess I never realized how much I compare myself to what I see online," I said. "Like, I know it's not all real, but it still makes me feel like I'm not enough sometimes. Like I should be trying to look more like that."

Miss Adler gave me a warm smile, the kind that made me feel like it was okay to say how I was really feeling. "Thank you for sharing that, Grace. It's really important that we talk about this because I think so many people feel the same way but don't always say it out loud."

She said that the truth is, none of us need to change to fit into someone else's idea of what we should look like. Beauty standards change all the time, and a lot of what we see in the media is about selling a product, not showing us what real people look like. It's important to remind ourselves that our value isn't tied to our appearance.

As the conversation moved on, I glanced at Lilly and Emma. They were both nodding, clearly thinking the same things I was. We'd had so many talks over the summer about being kinder to ourselves, about trying not to get caught up in what other people thought. But now, hearing it from Miss Adler, it felt like the pieces were starting to click into place.

I had known I shouldn't be comparing myself to people I saw

on screens. But I hadn't thought about it deeper than that. It's not about the filters or the sometimes fake, sometimes real stuff that's on there. It's deeper than that. The important part is that the photos and videos are focusing on the wrong things to begin with.

That night, when I got home, I told my mom about the discussion in class. She listened, nodding as she chopped vegetables for dinner. Mom said, "I'm glad your teacher is talking about this," "It's so important to remember that real beauty comes from how we treat ourselves and others—not from fitting into some impossible standard."

Standards, again! I started googling more about beauty standards after dinner, and I couldn't believe how much was out there. I looked at beauty standards from past decades and from other cultures, and after awhile, I realized that Miss Adler and Mom were right. There's no one definition of beauty, so why are we so obsessed with looking a certain way?

Mirror of Me: My Power Board Collage

Working in small groups or by yourself, create a body acceptance collage using magazine cutouts, drawings, and words that represent a healthy and confident body image. Then, answer the prompts.

What images, words, or quotes did you include to make yourself feel empowered and confident?

Emma, Lilly and I worked on our own collages, but together. Our collages had all kinds of things. We used magazine pictures of people with different body shapes, sizes, and abilities. Lilly found a photo of a softball player, and Emma picked a soccer player. I found a picture of someone dancing because that's something I love to do—it reminds me of how lucky I am to move my body. We also added some words like Strong and Brave. I found a picture of a smiling kid in a wheelchair, which made me think of some of Anna's friends. I wish she were here to help with this—she always knows how to say something that makes me think differently.

But honestly, it was hard to even think this way while making the collage. I kept wondering what everyone else was thinking about their own bodies. Emma was so confident when she found her pictures, like she didn't even have to try. And Lilly, well, she pretended not to care, but I could tell she was being careful about what she picked, almost like she didn't want anyone to notice too much.

The boys in our group were kind of a mixed bag. One of them said, "Why are we even doing this? No one cares about body acceptance for guys." At first, I wanted to roll my eyes, but then I thought about how it must be hard for them, too, in a different way. Another boy found a picture of a superhero and said, "This is what I'd want to look like," and we all just kind of nodded. It made me realize how much pressure everyone feels, even if we don't talk about it.

Why do you think body acceptance is important?

I think body acceptance is important because so many people, including me, spend way too much time feeling like they're not good enough. It's hard to look at yourself and not see all the things you wish were different. But I'm starting to think that maybe if we practiced being kinder to ourselves—even when it feels weird—it could help us be kinder to other people, too.

What did you learn from this activity?

I learned that everyone has their own struggles with how they see their body, even if they don't say it out loud. Emma might seem like she has it all together, but that doesn't mean she doesn't have doubts. And Lilly—I could tell she's still figuring out how to feel okay about herself, just like me. Even the boys surprised me. I never thought about how much pressure they might feel to look a certain way.

I also learned that body acceptance isn't about pretending to love everything about yourself all the time. It's more about finding little things to appreciate and being okay with not being perfect.

How did your group work together to create the collage?

We worked together okay, I guess, but it wasn't perfect. Emma kind of took charge, which is fine because she's good at that, but sometimes it felt like she wasn't really listening to anyone else's ideas. Lilly was quieter than usual, and I think she was uncomfortable. The boys mostly joked around, but they did end up contributing some good pictures in the end.

It wasn't exactly smooth, but I think that's normal. We're all so different—what we like, what we're comfortable with, how we see ourselves. But in the end, we made something that shows how important it is to accept and celebrate all those differences.

AFFIRMATIONS
Be Strong!
BREATHE
YOU
ARE
BRAVE
GRACE AND
GRATITUDE

November 27

Dear Diary,

My birthday is coming up, and I should be excited, right? But honestly, I don't really know how I feel about it. It's not that I don't want to do something, it's just... I don't know. I don't feel like making a big deal out of it. Should I invite anyone other than Anna, Emma and Lilly. People say "we should hang out" all the time, but when it comes down to it, does anyone really mean it? I guess part of me is scared that if I invited everyone, I'd just end up sitting there, waiting for people who never show.

I told Mom I didn't want a party, and suggested doing something chill just me and the girls, like seeing a movie at the mall, then grab dinner at that new sushi place in the food court. She even said they could sleep over if I wanted. That made me feel better, having some kind of plan. Mom always finds a way to make things special, even when I don't know what I want.

I think I'll go with it. A small party. No pressure. Just the people I actually *want* to be there.

November 29

Dear Diary,

Here's the thing: I'm trying to feel better about myself, I really am. But it's hard. I can't help but compare myself to everyone else. Even when I tell myself it's not real, I feel like I don't measure up. Like no matter what I do, I'll never look the way I think I'm supposed to. This week, Miss Adler talked about how the media shows us impossible standards, and that helped a bit. But still, when I look in the mirror, I see a body that feels too awkward, too different. My legs are too long, my hips feel weird, and I don't have abs like I see on magazine covers. I know I shouldn't think like that, but it's hard to ignore.

Writing it down makes it feel so real—like I can't escape it. But it also helps to get the words out of my head so I can see them on paper. It's been a while since I've looked in my special mirror and just gotten comfortable with my reflection. It seems like when I stop doing it for a while, I go right back to where I started a few months ago: Miserable.

I'm going to do that right now, actually. Please hold.

Phew. I'm back. It wasn't comfortable, especially at first. I saw the sticky note with the reminder that being myself is my superpower, but I didn't look too super. Still, I didn't put the mirror away. Instead, I did some deep breathing like Stella told us to try when we're feeling upset. Then, I tried to just... be with myself. When I tried that, something unexpected happened. In the glass, it almost seemed like my reflection seemed to shift—not physically, but in how it felt. It was like the mirror wanted me to see something deeper. For just a moment, I saw myself differently: not as the girl standing there awkwardly picking herself apart, but as someone standing tall, confident, her arms raised high in victory after scoring a basket. My heart caught in my chest. Could that really be me?

I blinked, and the image softened back to my reflection. I wasn't sure what had just happened, but I felt a tiny flicker of something I hadn't felt in a long time: hope. It was like the mirror had shown me a glimpse of who I could be if I stopped being so hard on myself—if I believed in myself the way Lilly, Emma, and Stella had been encouraging me to do. Maybe Emma was right in a way. Maybe I didn't really try that hard at tryouts because deep down, I didn't really believe I could succeed. But maybe that was because I don't actually want to be a basketball player. Maybe I want to do something else?

I thought about all the amazing women athletes I'd been watching lately—basketball players, soccer stars, dancers, Olympic gymnasts. They didn't all look like the influencers on Instagram either. But they were strong. Powerful. They moved their bodies in ways that inspired me, made me want to move mine too.

Maybe, I thought, my body didn't have to look a certain way to be good enough. Maybe it just had to be strong and capable, like theirs. And maybe, just maybe, I could love it for that.

It isn't about being perfect—it is about learning to be okay with who I am, no matter what the world tries to tell me. And with people like Lilly, Emma, Anna, Miss Adler, and my mom on my side, I know I don't have to face it alone.

December 2

Dear Diary,

I finally texted the girls about my birthday. I kept it casual —"Hey, thinking of seeing a movie and getting sushi on Friday, wanna come?"—so if they don't want to, it won't be a big deal. At least, that's what I *told* myself. But the second I hit send, I felt that weird nervous feeling in my stomach, like waiting for a reply would somehow decide whether this birthday is a good one.

Anna texted back right away—she's in for the movie and dinner, but she can't sleep over, which I guess I expected. That made me feel much better, since even if it was just the two of us, I know we'd still have fun. Plus, I was nervous her mom wouldn't let her come out to the mall at all. I know she's pretty protective and Anna can't always participate in group stuff. The others took longer to reply, but eventually, Lilly and Emma both said yes. No one seemed over-the-moon excited, but at least they're coming, and they're going to sleep over! It's been a while since we just had a girls night.

Mom's already talking about making a special breakfast the morning after if the sleepover happens. She does this thing where she makes pancakes in whatever shape you want. Last year, she made a heart, a star, and something that was *supposed* to be a cat but looked more like a blob. Maybe this birthday won't be so bad after all.

December 4

Dear Diary,

Tomorrow's my birthday. It's weird—I always imagine it feeling different the night before, like something magical is about to happen, but really, it's just another day.

I'm trying not to overthink it, but a tiny part of me still wonders if someone's going to back out at the last second. Last year, I went outside of my comfort zone and invited all the girls from my class and some of the neighborhood girls from the Hillcrest school down the road from ours. My mom had introduced me to these girls this past summer, since she's in a book club with their moms. We are all slightly different ages: Amy and Jessica are a few years younger than me, and Shauna is two years older than me. I went to Amy's birthday in the summer, it was a big party with all our families. A bunch of people came, but four girls from my class (including Jenny) texted me an hour before my party to say that they couldn't come... and then later, I saw them post a picture of them getting their nails done together instead of being at my party. That hurt! The party was still fun, but seeing that post, I felt like I was a second choice for *everyone*. This year, inviting only my three closest friends feels safer, but I still feel like I'm waiting for the text where one of them tells me they aren't coming.

Mom could tell I was spiraling a little, so she came into my room and sat on my bed. "You know," she said, "birthdays aren't about who shows up. They're about celebrating you and that can happen no matter what." She hugged me, and I let out this huge sigh, but it felt like I was releasing all these bad feelings, in a good way.

She's right. No matter what happens tomorrow, I'm going to enjoy it. Even if it's just sushi, a movie, and pancakes shaped like blobs.

December 6

Dear Diary,

My birthday was great! Mom surprised me by secretly inviting Amy, Shauna and Jessica as well, and they all met us at the mall. We saw the movie (it was okay, but honestly, the best part was whispering dumb jokes to the girls the whole time). Dinner was fun too. I don't think I'll ever get used to sushi, but the girls dared me to try wasabi, and let's just say I definitely regretted that decision. My mouth was on fire for five whole minutes.

I was a little nervous introducing Anna to Emma and Lilly, but since the other girls were there too, it felt more like a casual meeting rather than a serious friendship summit. I guess I was also a little nervous Anna would end up becoming better friends with them than me, but she actually seemed a little shy in our group. It all was fine, but I guess she's not used to being around a bunch of girls in a loud place like the mall. I hope they get a chance to get to know each other better at some point, but at least they seemed like they were getting along!

Only Emma and Lilly slept over, which felt just like the old days. We used to always have sleepovers since we live so close to each other, but we haven't done it since last summer so we were overdue. As usual, we stayed up way too late talking about nothing in particular and rewatching our favorite movies while trying to stay awake. Mom even made us pancakes again in the morning, so it's been a pancake-heavy couple days, but I'm not complaining. It was good to see Emma back to her normal eating at dinner and at breakfast—I guess that talk Miss Adler gave us last month really stuck with her!

Birthday presents! I almost forgot. Lilly and Emma got me a really great cozy sweatsuit—matching top and bottom—in a really nice sort of grown-up purple color. I love it, and I said it might be my new lucky sweatsuit, which made Anna laugh. Anna got me a pickleball paddle and a few balls, which I'm excited about. She's been telling me she wants me to start playing since it's a sport that she really likes doing when she feels good, so I guess I'll try it for her! Dad loves to play pickleball so I'm sure he can show me the basics. And Mom and Dad got me a gift certificate to my favorite jewelry store in the mall so I can pick out a pair of earrings that I like, which was really thoughtful of them. Mom says at my age, my style is changing all the time so she wanted me to find something I'm happy with, not something that she thought looked like me.

December 10

Dear Diary,

Today tested my patience. Jenny barely looked at me during science class, and when I finally worked up the courage to ask if I'd done something, she just shrugged and went back to laughing with Graham. We're all in a group together the next few days, which makes everything worse. It's like I'm invisible. Or worse, like I'm the one no one wants there but no one says it out loud.

When I got home, I couldn't take it anymore. I cranked up my favorite playlist, closed my door, and danced. At first, it was awkward, like my body forgot how to move. But then the beat kicked in, and I just went for it. Twirling, jumping, throwing my hands in the air like an idiot.

And you know what? It felt amazing. For the first time all day, I didn't feel judged. I wasn't worried about Jenny or my mom or anyone else. It was just me and the music.

I think I'll do it again tomorrow.

cerember 12

Dear Diary,

Anna has been getting a few day passes from the hospital so she can spend some afternoons out, which is really exciting. Her treatment has been going better than anyone expected, and she says they're even talking about her maybe being able to come to school next year instead of being homeschooled! But since she is allowed out, I'm going to bring her to Emma's basketball game on Monday. They played against Hillcrest and won, so now they are off to the semi-finals.

Anna hasn't met anyone at school other than Emma and Lilly, so I am excited to bring her with me and Lilly. She was so excited when I texted her, and said she is going to wear her lucky hoodie and is ready to cheer. I don't think I have a lucky hoodie? I have never really believed in things being "lucky," but I guess if people have moments of greatness or happiness with something on, it might feel lucky? Or maybe it's the opposite: wearing something you think is going to bring you luck ends up being lucky just because you believed in it. I admire Anna for the fact that despite being sick, she still believes in luck.

December 15

Dear Diary,

I'm so excited that Anna is coming to watch Emma's basketball game with me and Lilly today—Anna's mom is going to come with us to keep an eye on her, but Anna says she talked her into sitting a couple rows behind us so we don't notice she's there. It feels like everyone's buzzing about the game, and I'm getting all the feels. The energy is building, and we haven't even left yet.

I know it's Emma's big moment, and I just want everything to go perfectly for her. She's worked so hard for this, and I can already picture the way her face will light up if she plays well. (And I know how hard it will be for her if it doesn't go well. I think sometimes she takes it a little too seriously.)

Having Anna come with us makes it feel even more fun and like a bigger deal—I know she'll be cheering louder than anyone, probably embarrassing us all, but in the best way. And Lilly? She's already planning some ridiculous cheers that are guaranteed to make us laugh until we can't breathe. I can totally see her coming up with some over-the-top chant that no one else in the gym understands, but she'll fully commit to it anyway.

Mostly, I just hope Emma feels how much we all believe in her. No matter what happens, we'll be right there, screaming, laughing, and making memories.

December 16

Dear Diary,

We won! We won! Of course we won. Emma was on fire yesterday. I am so happy for her, she worked so hard for this. The game ended up going into overtime and we were all at the edge of our seats.

During games like that they are always playing really motivating music. I heard my favorite song and it put me in such a good mood, Lilly and Anna and I were all just singing along and I didn't care at all if anyone could hear us or thought we were cringy, we were just so happy. And it was great to see Lilly and Anna getting along so well. They bonded, but I didn't feel like I was getting left out or left behind. And when Emma came over after the game we were all jumping up and down and hugging and cheering and it was amazing. Anna was definitely tired after and her mom clearly wanted to get her home, but she looked really happy about spending time with us.

I came home and couldn't stop dancing around and singing it. Honestly, I think I'm onto something with these solo dance parties. They're my new secret weapon. Whenever I feel stressed or sad, I turn on my music and let myself move. It's like shaking off all the bad vibes.

Mom caught me dancing around today. I thought she'd yell

at me for having the volume up so loud, but instead, she just smiled and said she used to do the same thing when she was my age. Then she joined in! I swear, seeing my mom do a shoulder shimmy was the funniest thing ever.

What Does Self-Acceptance Mean to You?

Self-acceptance is all about recognizing that no one is perfect (not even movie stars or influencers!). We all have our strengths and weaknesses, and that's what makes us unique. Embrace all of it, because it's what makes you—you. It's okay if it's not easy at first. Just take it one day at a time. And hey, we're in this together, so let's keep practicing kindness to ourselves!

STEP 1: THINK ABOUT YOUR BODY.

Take a moment to think about the things your body can do, instead of how it looks. Write down three things you appreciate about your body. They can be small or big, but focus on the things that make your body awesome for what it can do!

I can dance around for a whole song, and I love how strong my body feels when I'm moving.

My hands are good at writing and drawing, and they help me express my thoughts in creative ways.

I can listen to my body and rest when I need to, which helps me take care of myself

STEP 2: REFLECT ON YOUR ACTIVITIES.

What's one way your body helps you enjoy something you love to do—whether it's a sport, a hobby, or just having fun? It can be anything, as long as it's something that makes you feel good about what your body can do. Example: "My legs help me run fast during soccer" or "My hands help me play the piano."

> When I write or draw, my hands and fingers help me create the stories and pictures that I love. It feels like my body is working with me to bring my ideas to life, and that makes me feel proud.

STEP 3: SET AN INTENTION.

Think about the next time you start comparing yourself to others. What's one kind or positive thing you'll tell yourself? It could be a reminder that your body is awesome, just as it is, and helps you do the things you love.

Examples: "I don't need to look like anyone else. I'm strong and amazing just as I am!" or "My body helps me do things I enjoy, and that's enough." or "I'm proud of the way I take care of my body."

> Next time I start comparing myself to others, I'll remind myself that I don't need to look like anyone else. My body does amazing things, and that's enough.

December 19

Dear Diary,

I've been thinking a lot about sports lately. For the longest time, I just assumed I wouldn't be good at them because I felt like I didn't belong—like I didn't have the right kind of body to be an athlete. I'm not tall like Emma, so how could I possibly be good at basketball? But maybe I've been holding myself back. Lately, I've been watching more amazing women athletes on TV and following them on social media, and I'm starting to feel like maybe I could be good at a sport too. Maybe sports aren't just for girls who are perfect athletic looking. Maybe they're for all of us.

I've been thinking a lot about how much I've been having fun dancing around my room listening to music lately. It makes me happy and it makes me feel good about myself. Maybe dance is something I could try as a sport instead of following Emma and Lilly to whatever activity they're doing. But I also want to get good enough at pickleball that I can play with Anna, so we have an activity we can do together. And then, there's the sports we're playing at school every day that aren't competitive. There's intramural volleyball happening at recess and I've been scared to join in, even though I used to really like playing volleyball a couple years ago. But I always talk myself out of it because I don't want to miss the ball and embarrass myself. But what if instead of getting stressed about any of those sports, I just remind myself that I don't have to be perfect at any of it? I just have to try. That's enough. Maybe next week I will try volleyball and see how it goes!

December 22

Dear Diary,

Today, I went to school with a new sense of determination: I was going to play volleyball intramurals after lunch. Walking into the gym, I got freaked out. It sort of felt like I was at basketball tryouts all over again... I was nervous and I almost turned and walked away, but I went in. As I walked into the gym, my stomach did a nervous flip, but I tried to remember the way I saw myself in the mirror and the decision I made: *I just have to try.* That's enough.

The game was intense, and I definitely wasn't the best player on the court. But something felt different about this compared to basketball tryouts. Instead of worrying about how I looked or whether I was good enough, I focused on how it felt to move my body. I wasn't as fast or as skilled as some of the other girls, but I realized that didn't matter as much as I thought it would. What mattered was that I was here, doing something I never thought I could do.

By the end of the game, I was sweaty and exhausted, but I felt proud of myself. I had pushed past my fears. I had stopped comparing myself to others, at least for a little while, and that was something. And I got the ball over the net a few times! It didn't feel quite as fun as dancing, but I had a good time, and the other girls high-fived me when we were done.

Later that day, back in class, Miss Adler pulled me aside. "I heard you joined in at volleyball intramural," she said with a smile.

I nodded, still feeling a bit unsure of how it all went—and a little embarrassed that she noticed. "Yeah... I'm not sure if I'll do it again, though."

Miss Adler's eyes sparkled. "Well, the important part is that you tried," she said. "You challenged yourself, and that's what matters. Whether you decide to try again or not, you should be really proud of yourself."

It feels like I've taken a big step today. Maybe it's not about looking a certain way or being the best at something. Maybe it's just about showing up, being kind to myself, and seeing where that takes me.

I told my mom about the game. She listened carefully, nodding along as I talked about the nerves, the excitement, and the relief I felt at the end. "I'm so proud of you, Grace, for trying something new," she said, and gave me a big hug. "No matter what, you should be proud too."

And I really am.

December 24

Dear Diary,

Wow! Somehow, it's already Christmas Eve! This is the downside of having a birthday in December: It all happens so fast. We've gotten so much snow, and it is one of those years where we only had two days off before Christmas from school... so I tried to use that time to my advantage and went tobogganing with Lilly yesterday. Emma had to do extra practices so she couldn't come, but we had fun anyway!

Now, I'm sitting by the window ledge where the tree is, the lights are twinkling, and the house smells like cinnamon and pine. I'm really excited for tomorrow—family time, the gifts, the food (can't forget about the cookies!)—but at the same time, there's this weird feeling in my chest. It's kind of like a mix of happy and sad, and I don't even know why.

I've always loved the holidays, but this year feels a little different. Maybe it's because I've been seeing people on social media posting all their "perfect" snowy photos, and it's like they're all having this magical time.. I know we talked about how social media comparison isn't helpful and all of that, but it's hard *not* to compare sometimes.

I also always normally go with Mom to the mall to get a new outfit for the holidays. It's sort of our little tradition. I know it's not a big deal, but it makes me feel more confident when I have something new to wear, like a little piece of me that feels special. This year, though, things have been busy, and since I only had two days off before Christmas, we didn't get to go. I don't want to make a big deal out of it, but I kind of feel even more off now. I know I am going to see everyone post their holiday pictures in all these cool new outfits and I don't have something new to wear—or super cute holiday themed pajamas, which is what a lot of girls post.

Mom did make me feel a bit better after dinner by telling me there were a few surprise presents she thought I'd like and she hoped would fit, so I hope that means she got me some cute stuff. Not many girls can say that their moms have good taste in outfits for them, but my mom is weirdly good at picking things out that I like! And yes, I know that the gifts and outfits aren't what Christmas is about. It's not about the perfect gifts, or the perfect tree, or the way everything looks in a photo. It's about being with the people you love and really *feeling* those moments. It's the hugs, the laughs, the inside jokes, the stories we tell around the table. It's about connecting, even when things aren't perfect. But I also can't wait to message Lilly, Emma and Anna in the morning to see what they got and show off my presents!

Some years, Christmas Eve is super hectic, but not this year. We had a pretty chill Christmas Eve since it was the off year for my cousins on my mom's side—they're her brother's kids. This year, they are at their family on their mom's side, so it was just Mom, Dad, Jake and I, and for once, Jake wasn't being super annoying. We watched our favorite classic Christmas movies and it felt so special and cozy. Jake has been so super excited since Halloween for Santa to come, so this night is like everything to him. We helped Mom bake cookies yesterday, and tonight we put them by our fireplace on this big Santa plate with carrots for the reindeer. I know I'm too old to really believe in Santa, but secretly I kind of do. I'd never say that to my friends, but I can tell you, Diary!

Tomorrow, my cousins are coming over after we open presents and have breakfast. I don't get to see them too often, but when I do we have the best time, so I am looking forward to that.

December 25

Dear Diary,

Phew! What a day. Christmas always feels like it takes forever to come, and then it's just *here*. This morning was full of everything I hoped it would be. Jake basically flew out of bed and ran down the stairs to see if Santa came. He screamed when he saw the bike, which was cute, and we opened presents in our pajamas with the fire on and cinnamon rolls in the oven.

I loved seeing everyone's reactions to the gifts I helped pick out, and even though I didn't have a new outfit this year, I wore my coziest red sweater and actually felt okay in it. Mom got me a great new coat, but since we were inside, I didn't really get to show it off to anyone.

And now, tonight, the house is quiet. The wrapping paper is stuffed in bags, and everyone's kind of doing their own thing. I'm still grateful for everything, especially the way the whole house smelled like cinnamon and roast turkey and the way my cousins and I laughed so hard we cried at the dinner table. But there's this weird heaviness in my chest again, kind of like that mix I felt yesterday: happy and something else. I think I get overwhelmed thinking about what comes next.

Like, now what? When I was scrolling on social media after dinner, I kept seeing people post things about goals and "new year, new me" already, and it's only been a few hours since

Christmas dinner. It feels like everyone's racing ahead and I can't even process how I feel right now.

I thought today would be all joy, but after the presents got opened and we had breakfast, I kept catching myself thinking, 'now what?'. Holidays are strange like that. I guess they can hold both happiness and heaviness at the same time. Before I started writing in you, Diary, I pulled out one of the mindful cards that Stella gave us last time she visited our class. The one I grabbed talked about box breathing and how it can help calm your mind when you're stuck in your head or feeling overwhelmed. So, I tried it. I sat in my room, lit my little tree lights, and just breathed. Four counts in. Four counts hold. Four counts out. Four counts hold. Repeat. It didn't fix everything, but I actually felt more grounded after, like my feet were on the floor again. I think I'm going to use these cards more often. Maybe I'll even bring them into the new year with me instead of making a huge list of resolutions I probably won't keep. One calm breath at a time feels like enough for now.

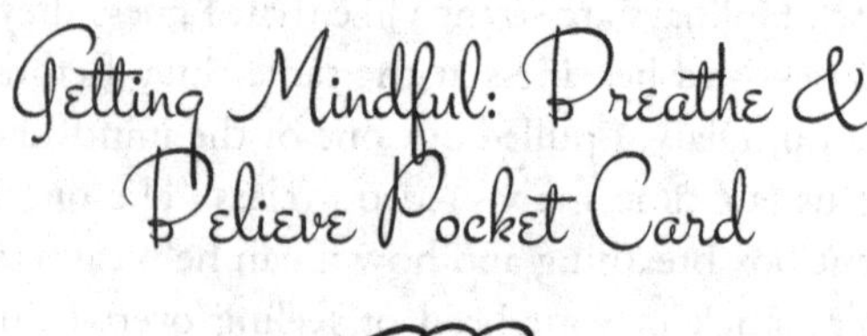

Getting Mindful: Breathe & Believe Pocket Card

A great way to practice mindfulness is through box breathing, which can help you feel calmer and more focused.

Here's how to get started with box breathing:

1. Sit comfortably in a quiet place with your back straight.
2. Breathe in through your nose for a count of four. (Imagine filling your lungs with air as if you're drawing air up into your chest.)
3. Hold your breath for a count of four. (Keep your chest full without feeling tense.)
4. Breathe out through your mouth for a count of four. (Release all the air slowly and fully.)
5. Hold your breath again for a count of four before starting the next round.
6. Repeat this cycle for four rounds, focusing on the rhythm of your breath.

Mindfulness is about paying attention to the present moment instead of getting stuck in the past or worrying about the future. It helps you notice your thoughts and feelings without judging them, and box breathing can help you tune in.

CREATE YOUR MINDFUL REMINDER:

Your Calm Word _________

Your Kind Action – Draw a small picture or describe the kind action you'll use (hand on heart, hug, etc.)."

Your Box Breathing Goal – I will practice mindful breathing ___ times a week to help with _________ (e.g., nerves before a game, stressful moments, etc.)."

Whenever you feel overwhelmed, stressed, or just need a moment to reset, try box breathing to reconnect with yourself!

December 27

～❧～

Dear Diary,

It's that strange time between Christmas and New Year's where I don't even know what day it is. Everything feels like a blur of leftovers, holiday movies, and staying in pajamas way too long. The tree is still up, the lights are still twinkling, but the excitement of Christmas morning has settled. It's kind of nice, though. No pressure, no rush—just days that feel like they don't quite belong to anything.

I've spent most of today catching up with girls about their family Christmas'. And honestly? It seems like everyone had the same feelings I did. Opening presents, family, food, all that stuff was really fun, but then—boom!—it's over and that's a strange feeling.

I thought I was over it, but I still felt a little weird this morning. It's hard to explain, but it's like Christmas came and went so fast, and now I'm left with this... I don't know, empty feeling? I love the holidays, but sometimes when they're over, I feel this mix of sadness and restlessness, like I should be *doing* something. It's like I'm in between—between one year and the next, between the excitement of Christmas and whatever comes next.

Maybe I just need a plan for tomorrow. I might ask Lilly or Emma if they want to go skating or do something outside. Or maybe I'll just take the day to reset—clean my room, journal, figure out what I want for the new year. Speaking of the new year, I should probably find something to wear for New Year's Eve, since I didn't get any new holiday outfits for Christmas time. I know I shouldn't complain because I do have plenty of clothes, but the Get Ready With Me videos that all the girls seem to be posting for New Years really have me wanting a shopping spree.

December 29

Dear Diary,

I told Mom that I really missed having a new outfit for the holidays, while still trying to sound grateful for my coat and for my whole closet full of clothes. But the truth is, I have outgrown a lot of my fancier dresses and pants from the last year so I did kind of need some new stuff. Mom agreed once we went through my closet together (and pulled out a bag of clothes that I could donate). And then we finally went shopping today for a New Year's Eve outfit. I was so excited at first—it's our little tradition, even if we didn't get to do it before Christmas this year. But somewhere between the racks of sparkly tops and the piles of jeans I tried on that didn't fit quite right, the excitement kind of faded. It was like the idea of shopping was exciting but the reality didn't quite work.

I don't know why, but shopping always seems to bring out this side of me I don't like. The side that overthinks everything. The side that picks apart the way I look in the mirror instead of just enjoying the clothes. Every time I pulled something over my head, I found something wrong with it. Too tight. Too loose. Too sparkly. Too plain. The way the waist bunched weird. The way my arms looked. Ugh.

Mom could tell I was getting frustrated. "It's supposed to be fun," she reminded me, holding up a dress she thought I'd like. I nodded, but I couldn't shake the feeling. It's not even really about the clothes, I think. It's more about how I feel about *me* in them.

After what felt like a million tries, I found something—a simple black top with little shimmer and some comfy jeans that actually felt good. It wasn't the most show-stopping thing ever, but when I put it on, I didn't immediately start listing things I didn't like. And maybe that's enough.

On the way home, Mom got us hot chocolates, and we drove past houses still glowing with Christmas lights still. As we sipped our hot chocolates, the warmth from the cup slowly melted away some of the frustration I'd been holding onto. The lights outside blurred past the car window, little reminders that the holiday season wasn't quite over yet.

Maybe I didn't find the *perfect* outfit, but I did find something that felt comfortable—something that felt *like me*. And maybe that's what I need to take into the new year. Less pressure to look a certain way, less comparing, and more moments like this. Just being here, in the glow of twinkling lights, feeling okay with where I am.

It's almost New Year's Eve. A fresh start. And I think I'm ready for it.

January 1

Dear Diary,

I have to admit, even though I get stressed about resolutions and everyone declaring New Year, New Me, I am still a little obsessed with New Years. How fun is it to just get to shout '3...2...1... *Happy New Year!*' and feel that sense of a new beginning? Mom and Dad had their friends over, and all their kids were here too, and that included Lilly and her parents! (Emma would have come but she had to go spend the holiday at her cousins' place.) It was chaos in the best way, with balloons everywhere and sparklers lighting up the backyard.

As we counted down to midnight, I couldn't help but make the same wish I always do: for this year to finally be *my* year. The year where all my anxious thoughts disappear and I wake up every day feeling confident, like those girls who seem to have it all figured out.

The year where I figure out who I am and what I want.

Lilly and I talked about resolutions earlier in the night while we were eating way too many chocolate-covered pretzels. She said hers is to try out for the softball team. "What about you, Grace?" she asked, her face lit up by the string lights.

I froze for a second because, honestly, I wasn't sure that 'finding myself' felt like a very good resolution. After everything last year—basketball tryouts and not making the team, school stress, and figuring out how to like myself more—I wasn't sure if I was ready to make *another* big promise to myself, especially in front of someone else. But then I blurted out, "I just want to be less scared of things."

It felt so small compared to Lilly's goal, but she smiled and said, "That's a big deal, Grace. And you're already braver than you think."

Maybe she's right. I mean, I've done some scary things this past year—trying out for basketball even though I was terrified, speaking up in class when I usually stay quiet, and learning to enjoy volunteering. But there's still a part of me that worries I'm going to slip back into old habits, like hiding or doubting myself.

So, here's my resolution, Diary: this year, I'm going to try to keep moving forward, even when it's hard. I'm going to remind myself of what the mirror showed me—that I'm capable of more than I think. Maybe that doesn't mean my anxious thoughts will disappear overnight, but I can learn to face them, one at a time.

And I didn't say this one to Lilly, but my other goal is definitely to find a sport that I actually like. Having fun playing volleyball made me think that there is a sport for me out there, I just haven't figured out exactly what it is yet.

Lilly and I stayed up way too late after everyone else went to bed, talking about all the things we want to do this year. By the time we crashed on the couch, I felt a little spark of hope, like maybe this really *could* be my year.

Happy New Year!

January 5

Dear Diary,

Back to school, back to the same old routine. It's only been a week, but winter break feels like it was a lifetime ago—it's funny how quick the New Year mentality starts to fade away. But today, Miss Adler was waiting for us first thing in the morning with her "Welcome Back!" sign... and an assignment on our desks. Not even one day to ease back in—classic.

The day started fine. Lilly and I walked to school together, crunching over the icy sidewalk and joking about how we'd rather be back in bed. We were both excited to see Emma, but the second we got to our lockers, something felt... off. Emma was already surrounded by a group of girls I don't know very well, and they were all laughing about something on her phone.

"Hey, you made it!" Emma said when she saw us, but then she went right back to showing off whatever was on her screen. Lilly leaned over to me and whispered, "Guess we're not the only ones who missed her."

I laughed, but it didn't feel funny.

And then, in math class, Emma sat with those girls instead of us. I tried not to let it bother me, but it did. Every time she turned around to whisper something to them, I felt this weird ache in my chest, like maybe we weren't enough for her anymore. What happened over the holiday?

At lunch, things got worse. Someone at the table started talking about New Year's resolutions, and it turned into a competition about who was going to work out the most or eat the "healthiest." I hate these conversations. They always make me feel like I don't belong, like I'm supposed to be keeping score on how many salads I eat or how many sit-ups I can do.

Emma was all-in, saying she's been doing this workout app every morning. "It's actually fun," she said, smiling like it was no big deal. Lilly tried to change the subject to softball tryouts, but no one listened. I just sat there, poking at my sandwich and wishing I could disappear.

I don't know why I let this stuff get to me. Emma's allowed to have other friends, and it's not like I want to be the kind of person who cares about who's trying what diet or doing a workout streak. But sitting there, listening to everyone talk about what they're doing to "glow up" this year, I couldn't help but feel like I'm already falling behind.

After school, Lilly and I walked home in silence for a while. She must've noticed I was upset because she finally said, "Emma's just excited about her new friends. She's not ditching us, Grace."

I nodded, but the ache didn't go away. And honestly, Lilly didn't exactly sound sure of herself either.

When I got home, I sat down with the mirror again. I didn't really want to look at myself, but I forced myself to anyway. The reflection stared back, and for a second, I thought I saw that same confident version of me I'd seen before. But it flickered, and all I could see was regular old Grace—awkward, unsure, and not enough.

I know it's just one bad day, but I hate feeling like this. Like I'm stuck between who I was and who I'm trying to become.

January 7

Dear Diary,

This morning, Mom brought up something kind of unexpected.

We were just sitting at the kitchen table—me, halfway through my peanut butter toast, and her, scrolling through something on her iPad while sipping her usual green tea—when she looked up and told me she saw a weekend dance camp pop-up at the dance school in town. Then, she asked if I wanted to go. I almost choked on my toast. "Me? Dance camp?"

She smiled that annoying all-knowing mom-smile she does when she's trying to plant a seed without making it too obvious. She said it's just for a weekend. All different styles—hip hop, lyrical, even some fun fusion stuff. She promised no ballet.

Ballet. The pink tights, tight buns, and tiptoeing in a room full of mirrors. She put me into a class a couple of years ago after I begged to try it, and I think I lasted two months before I begged to quit! It always felt like everyone else knew how to move like floating butterflies while I just...flopped. Mom didn't push back then, which I appreciated. I think she could tell I wasn't feeling it.

But today, she was talking about how she noticed I've been dancing around my room more and that I look happy. She said something that made me smile, "When I see you dancing around, it's like your body just knows what it wants to do... Maybe this

156

could be something you try again, on your terms this time." She said with a sort of questioning look on her face.

She wasn't being pushy. It felt more like an invitation. A "maybe this could be fun" kind of thing.

And the truth is, I have been dancing in my room. A lot. Not to perform, not for anyone else, just... because it feels good. Like my body is speaking a language I don't even have to think about and it gets my mind off of things blasting music.

So maybe I'll go. Just to see. I'm not sure what will come of it. Could this be my thing?

$$\mathcal{January\ 9}$$

Dear Diary,

This morning wasn't awful, but it wasn't great either. Just one of those days where you float through school feeling like you're there but not really present. At least, until science class. Then it was awful.

In science, we got assigned to groups for a big project on ecosystems—ours is the marine ecosystem, meaning oceans. But guess who's in mine? Emma... and Jenny. Yes, that Jenny. The queen of snark and subtle eye rolls. The second our science teacher Mrs. Kent called out our names, I swear Jenny let out the tiniest groan, just loud enough for me to hear.

Emma, of course, jumped right in, offering to take the lead and organize everything. She's so good at that kind of stuff— taking charge, making it look easy. I felt like a shadow sitting there, just nodding and pretending I wasn't hyper-aware of every move Jenny made. At one point, Jenny even said, "Do you think Grace will actually get that done?" as Emma was trying to divide the project up between us and was giving me the research on different types of plants that grow in salt water. She said it with this fake little laugh, like it was a joke. But it wasn't.

I wanted to say something back, but the words got stuck in my throat. I just stared at my notebook, wishing I could disappear. Emma didn't stand up for me either, just kind of pretended she didn't hear Jenny.

At lunch, it didn't get much better. Emma sat with Jenny and her friends instead of us, and Lilly tried to play it cool, but I could tell she wasn't happy about it either. "She'll come back," Lilly said, biting into her apple like she didn't care, but I know her too well.

The thing is, I don't even blame Emma. She's been spending more time with those girls this week, and maybe she feels like they get her in ways Lilly and I don't since most of them are either on her basketball team or in some kind of school sport. Although a few of them are just cool and fashionable and somehow super trendy, like social media influencers but in real life. It's hard not to feel like we're being left behind.

When I got home, I meant to do some research for the project, but I couldn't focus. Instead, I sat in front of the magic mirror again, even though I didn't really want to. I stared at my reflection for a long time, half-hoping it would show me something.

At first, nothing happened. It was just me—tired, frustrated, overthinking everything. But then, I thought about what Stella said the last time she talked to the class: "Self-compassion isn't about fixing all your problems at once. It's about being kind to yourself, especially when you're struggling."

So, I tried. I took a deep breath and said, "You're allowed to feel upset, Grace. It doesn't mean you're failing." It felt weird, like I was pretending to be someone more confident than I am. But as I stared into the glass, I could almost see it—the version of me who doesn't let Jenny's comments stick, who speaks up even when it's scary.

I don't think I'm that person yet, but maybe I can try to be.

Goodnight, Diary.

January 11

Dear Diary,

Tonight was one of my favorite nights. It was just Mom and me, and we went out for dinner to this cozy little place I love. We decided to share a few different plates, just because we could, and it felt nice to just be with her, no distractions. I love my dad and my brother, but when it's just Mom and I, everything feels a little simpler. I know I'm really lucky she makes time for us to have these hangouts... the last time I mentioned one of our dinner dates to Lilly, she said she wished her mom would make time for her like this!

On the way home from dinner, Mom and I started really talking. I told her how I've been feeling a little left out lately—especially with Emma. Like she's moved on to this new group of friends, and Lilly and I are sort of... well, not really included anymore. It doesn't feel like she's doing it on purpose, but when you're not invited to hang out, it still stings. I don't know how to explain it, but it's like there's this invisible space growing between us, and it got even worse at the end of this week. I asked if she and Lilly wanted to hang out on Saturday at the park, and Lilly couldn't because she had to do a family thing, but Emma just said she had other plans. Then later, I heard her talking to Jenny and a few girls about hanging out at the mall. I half-expected her to then invite us to join her, but she didn't.

Mom was quiet for a second after I told her all of that, like she was thinking about what to say. Then, she told me a story about a childhood friend she used to be really close with. She said that at some point, their friendship just changed, kind of without either of them realizing it. One of them started drifting away, and they didn't talk as much, and eventually, they just didn't hang out the same way anymore. Mom didn't sound sad when she talked about it, though. She said that it wasn't about losing something, but more about how sometimes people change, and that's just part of life. Friendships can evolve, and it doesn't mean it's the end.

I wasn't sure if that helped. I guess change is normal, but sometimes it doesn't make it hurt any less. It still feels like Emma was slipping away, even though she's not being mean or anything. It was just... a missed invitation. She and her new group of friends planned something, and Lilly and I weren't part of it. It wasn't like Emma was actively excluding us, but she wasn't including us either, and it felt weird. I wish she'd at least texted, like she used to.

So, I decided to try something right then and there. I sent Emma a message, just to invite her to do something small: Walking home together after school and stopping at the mini mart to get our favourite candy on the way. I sort of assumed that she'd say yes, and I'd realize that the whole problem was all in my head. But she declined. She said she was walking home with her basketball girls.

That really stung. I guess change isn't always easy to accept, even when you know it's a part of life. But maybe Mom's right. Maybe change doesn't always mean loss. Maybe it's just another chapter. And even if Emma and I are growing apart a little, it doesn't mean I won't find new things to fill up the space. I mean, I do have new friends too, or at least, one new friend—Anna. And I don't always invite Emma and Lilly to hang out with us. In fact, I don't even think about inviting them! And I don't think I'm being mean. So maybe that's what's happening with Emma.

For now, I'm going to try to be okay with it. Not everything stays the same, and that's okay. I just have to keep moving forward, even if it's a little scary. And tomorrow morning, I'm going to try the Power Up routine that Stella gave us a while ago. I'm not sure it'll help me deal with Emma, but maybe?

Create Your Power Up Morning Routine

～

It only takes a few minutes to start your day on the right foot. Even making a few minutes for me-time can set a good tone for the day. Can you plan a five-minute morning routine that feels good for you?

Consider adding:

- Taking a few deep breaths (maybe doing a round of Box Breathing) right when you wake up
- Reading your Mirror Affirmation while brushing your teeth and washing your face
- Have a mini-dance party to a favorite song (get our fave playlist at StrongGirlPublishing.com/mirror)
- Get dressed, eat breakfast, head to school!

Make your morning routine plan here:

Okay, tomorrow I'm going to try something new with my morning routine. Stella says starting the day with positive vibes can totally change everything, so why not give it a shot? Here's my plan:
Start the day with 5 deep breaths
Look at my Mirror Mantra while brushing my teeth and washing my face. "Being Myself is My Superpower. And today is my day"
Music & Dance Party: Get dressed and turn on a fun playlist on Spotify. Dance around the room like I'm in a music video.
Pack bag, eat breakfast and grab essentials.

Afterwards, reflect on your new routine. How did it go?

So, I woke up, and instead of just rushing around like I usually do, I took my deep breaths, then stood in front of the mirror and said my morning mantra: "Being Myself is My Superpower." It gave me this boost, like I was ready to take on the day, even if it wasn't going to be perfect.
Then, I added in my favorite part—a little music! I turned on my Spotify pump up playlist and started dancing around my room like I was in a music video (not even kidding). The tunes were upbeat, and I could feel myself waking up, feeling happier and more ener-

gized. It's crazy how a little bit of dancing can totally change your mood!

Actually doing the routine really made a difference. I felt ready to take on whatever came my way today. Maybe this "power routine" isn't just some cheesy thing—it actually works. I think I'm going to make it a thing every morning. If I start my day with positivity, a little music, and a dance, it might just turn into a good day!

January 15

Dear Diary,

Today took a surprising turn, and maybe it was because of my new Power Up morning routine getting me in a better mood and showing up as someone a little bit brighter! After school, Emma, Jenny and I ended up walking home together. I wasn't even sure if Emma was going to say anything to me after how things have been lately, but she waved me over when she saw me near the bike racks, and just like that, we were walking like we used to... Except Jenny was there too. She actually came over to us because she wanted to check in on the poster for our project, but then we all just kind of started walking together naturally.

We talked about the poster and the project, and it was weird: Jenny and I actually had the same idea at the same time! We both blurted out that we should go to a pet store and get some actual salt water plants to have as a prop. We both looked horrified that we said basically the same thing, and it was an awkward moment, but then Emma started laughing and we both started giggling too. After that, we just fell into normal conversation, and some-where between chatting about a pop quiz and complaining about the cafeteria tacos, I mentioned that my mom made banana bread last night.

Emma's eyes lit up and she was like, "Wait, your mom's

banana bread? So good." Then she looked at Jenny and said something like, "We should stop by and try some!"

I was kind of caught, because on one hand, Jenny has been pretty mean to me all year, but I also didn't want to start a fight, so I just shrugged and told them to come over. So they came to my house! And my mom totally played it cool—I was so nervous she'd start yelling at Jenny for being mean to me, since just a few days ago I was telling Mom about all of our drama. But she just said something like, "Good thing I made banana bread this morning," and popped a plate of warm slices in front of us like it was all part of the plan.

And the crazy thing was that Jenny was weirdly... nice? Like, she was overly polite to Mom, and kept complimenting the banana bread like she was a food critic. "This is so moist. Did you add cinnamon? You can really taste it." I couldn't tell if she was being extra or if that's just her default setting. And she kept smiling at me too. Not in a fake way. More like in a "hey, we're cool" way. It completely threw me off. But sitting there, all three of us laughing about Jenny's over-the-top banana bread reviews, felt kind of normal again. Just for a little bit. Emma didn't say anything about not inviting me to the mall last weekend. It didn't come up at all, and I didn't want to bring it up and spoil a nice moment.

I still don't really know where I stand with Emma. Or Jenny, honestly. But today, it felt less confusing. And I'll take that.

Also... I should probably ask Mom for the actual banana bread recipe in case this happens again.

January 20

Dear Diary,

So, I've been doing the new morning thing for a few days now: deep breaths, mirror mantra, music, dancing around like it's my own private concert, and honestly? It really works. This morning as I was shimmying around the room to the beat, I thought about dance camp that Mom mentioned again, and instead of that voice in my head saying. "No way, not you," I heard a kinder voice in my head telling me to just try!

Over breakfast, I told Mom that I was thinking about going, and she said to just let her know and she'd sign me up. And then... it's going to sound weird, but I think I got a sign. During lunch at school, someone had left a flyer on the bulletin board near my locker. It was bright yellow and said: "Move like nobody's watching. March Break Dance Camp – All Levels Welcome." The same camp Mom talked about. I swear it hadn't been there before! I stopped and just stared at it for a second. Was the universe eavesdropping?

I guess I'm going to dance camp!

January 24

Dear Diary,

I've been thinking about Jenny more than I thought I would. After Thursday's banana bread thing, I kind of expected everything to go back to normal (whatever that even means anymore). But instead, it's like I can't stop wondering if I've been wrong about her. Or maybe not wrong, but just... not fully right.

I used to think Jenny was just one of those girls who always had something to prove. Loud. Confident. A little too perfect all the time. The kind of girl who knows exactly what lip gloss to wear and how to make friends out of thin air. The kind of girl who would never be nervous about anything—definitely not banana bread or awkward silences or how close you sit to someone at lunch.

But at my house the other day, she was different. Still confident, yeah, but not in a show-offy way. She was funny, and sort of dorky with her food commentary, and honestly? She was kind of... nice. To me. She complimented my mom, asked about the candle we had lit in the kitchen (who even notices that stuff?), and laughed at my joke about how the bananas were probably way too brown when my mom used them.

She even helped clear the plates. Jenny. The same Jenny who once rolled her eyes at cafeteria duty. And when she left, she thanked me and said she had fun! She didn't say it like it was just something to say. She looked at me when she said it. Like she meant it.

It made me realize—I don't actually know Jenny that well. Maybe I've just decided who she is in my head, based on the way she is with Emma, or how she walks into a room like she owns it. But maybe she's more than that. Maybe she's someone I could get to know... if I stop assuming things. And okay, maybe if she really does stop being mean to me and the other girls. But maybe I've been reading into her little remarks and assuming they're meaner than they actually are.

I mean, maybe I've done the same thing other people do to me—put her in a box without asking what's actually inside. It's weird. I don't know if we're friends now. But something's shifted. All last week, she was totally normal as we worked on the ecosystem project together. I did get a bunch of fake coral and saltwater plants from the pet store, and I was afraid she would think my idea of using toy plastics sharks and dolphins (that I stole from Jake's room) was too baby-ish, but she actually said it was a great idea and even said her dad had an old aquarium we might be able to use to set it all up and make a diorama type thing. I think we're going to have the best presentation in the whole class!

(Also, side note: I did get Mom's banana bread recipe. Just in case this turns into a regular thing.)

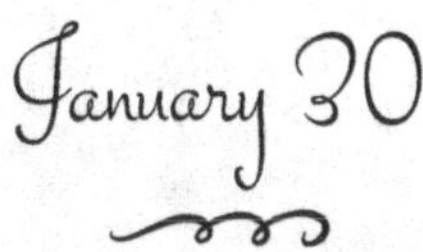

January 30

Dear Diary,

Today after school, I went over to the hospital with mom. She had to go for work, and Anna's been back there for the last week so I wanted to go say hi. She seemed to be doing really well, she had her energy back and was joking around with a couple of the other kids I now recognize from the floor when I got there. I swear, she's like the social queen of this wing of the hospital!

Anyway, our hangout somehow turned into us making up our own dance routine to post on social media. I don't even know how it happened—we were just playing music off my phone, and then Anna stood up and was like, "Okay, I'm choreographing." Five minutes later, we were both practically on the floor laughing. Her idea of choreography was this mix of dramatic arm movements and pretending to faint in slow motion, though it also kind of looked like a synchronized swimmer starting to go under water, and not in a way that would get a good score. Still, I followed along with her and the beat, and when both of us were doing it in perfect sync with the music, I think maybe it kind of worked!

One of the nurses peeked in and told us we should post it. We didn't (yet), but we promised we'd perfect it for next time.

I don't know—seeing Anna like that made me feel a little

lighter. Like even when things are hard, there's still space for silly fun. I think maybe she needed it. I know I did. Sometimes, it's the most random things that remind you that people are still here, still fighting, still them.

<h1 style="text-align:center">February 5</h1>

Dear Diary,

It's so weird how much things can change from one day to the next. The last time I saw Anna, just a few days ago, she was feeling good and energized. But not today. Anna wasn't herself at all when I visited her at the hospital. She's been there a while now, I guess, and normally she doesn't make a big deal out of spending time there, but today, I could tell the second I saw her that something was off. She was quieter, sort of zoned out. Normally she brings this spark, like her energy just fills the space, and when I come in, she jumps right into some random story, but today she just picked at her sandwich and stared at the table.

She told me things have been harder lately. She said her meds are making her super nauseous again, and she's frustrated because she finally felt like she was getting her energy back. She hates how up and down everything is. One week she feels strong enough to do everything, and the next she's curled in bed with headaches and no appetite. I can't even imagine how that must feel. She even told me that she wishes she could do half the things I can, which made me feel really sad for her.

She also said she's scared people are going to stop including her because she can't always show up. That broke my heart—I hoped she didn't think of me like that. She matters. A lot. I didn't know what to say to make it better, but I hope she felt even a little bit seen. Sometimes I forget that being strong doesn't mean pretending everything's fine. Anna's one of the strongest people I know, and today reminded me that even strong people need space to not be okay.

February 8

Dear Diary,

Even as I'm worried about Anna and how she's doing—I've been trying to send her silly memes and videos to cheer her up—I've been frantically working on the presentation with Jenny and Emma and trying to not freak out about it. Anna's bad day sort of put it in perspective, and I know it's not a big deal if I'm not perfect, but at the same time, I really don't want to be embarrassed in front of the class, and I've been daydreaming (day-night-maring?) about Jenny making fun of me and Emma being mad at me for messing up. They haven't been nervous at all. I swear, they're just excited and enjoying the whole thing!

Tomorrow is the big presentation, and I'm officially freaking out. Lilly tried to help today as I was going over our presentation and getting more and more nervous. Instead of going to lunch, I even went to the library just to get some quiet time to go over what I would have to say to the class. Lilly came barging into the library with her usual whirlwind energy and said, "Grace, I have the perfect solution for you: power posing!" Then she spread her feet apart, planted her hands on her hips, and puffed out her chest like a superhero. In the middle of the library! People were staring. I'm 99 percent sure I turned into a tomato.

She swears if I do it for one minute, I'll feel more confident—

she saw a video about it online from an actual scientist! She even printed out a worksheet she found about it to show me. I'm desperate enough to try it... but only in the privacy of my own room. Definitely not in public.

Wish me luck.

The Power of the Power Pose

Did you know that how you stand can actually change how you feel? A power pose is a confident, open stance that helps you feel strong, brave, and ready to take on anything. When you stand tall, your brain gets the message that you are powerful!

STEP 1: TRY A POWER POSE

Stand up and try one of these poses for 30 seconds to 1 minute. You can do this in front of a mirror or not—figure out which way works best for you!

- **Superhero Pose** – Stand with your feet shoulder-width apart, hands on your hips, chin up, and chest lifted.
- **Victory Pose** – Stand tall, stretch your arms up in a "V" shape, and imagine crossing the finish line of a big race!
- **Rockstar Pose** – Stand with your legs apart, one hand on your hip, and the other raised like you're about to take the stage.
- Any other pose that feels confident to you!

STEP 2: USE YOUR POWER POSE!

Whenever you need a confidence boost—before a big test, a sports game, or speaking in front of a group—try a power pose for **one minute.** It might feel silly at first, but science shows it can actually help!

Remember: *Confidence isn't just about how you feel on the inside—it's also about how you carry yourself on the outside. Stand tall, take up space, and own your power!*

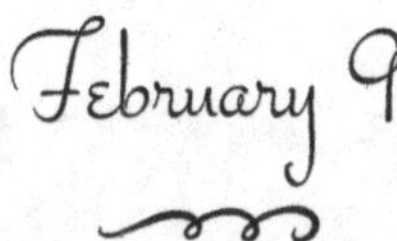

February 9

Dear Diary,

You are not going to believe this: The crazy power pose thing actually worked. Okay, fine, Lilly was right. I owe her. This morning, I locked myself in the bathroom and did the pose. Hands on hips, chin up, just like she said. At first, I felt ridiculous. But after a minute, I started to feel... different. Like maybe I wasn't just pretending to be confident. Maybe I *was* confident.

The presentation went way better than I thought it would. Sure, my hands were shaking, and my voice cracked a little, but I got through it. I even looked up from my notecards a few times! Luckily, Emma and Jenny did a lot of the talking since I had done a lot of work on the aquarium itself, but I didn't feel like they were judging me for not talking as much, or acting like they did more work. We just did different things that we're good at, and weirdly, I think we made a great team. Who would have thought?

And everyone—Mrs. Kent included—totally loved our aquarium. She even said she was going to leave it in the classroom on a shelf so we could all enjoy the marine ecosystem more. I guess I'm not the only one who loves cool water projects like this.

After class was over, we all high-fived, and for a minute, it felt like things with Emma were totally back to normal, and that maybe Jenny would actually become a friend. We even all sat at the same lunch table, even though Jenny mainly talked to her friends and I mainly talked to Lilly, and Emma sort of went between the groups. Maybe we can all be friends this way!

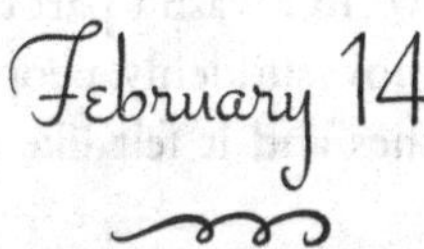

February 14

Dear Diary,

Valentine's Day in the younger grades was easier. You had to give everyone a card, so no one got left out. You'd go home with a paper bag full of cheap candy and folded-up notes with "You rock!" written in bubble letters. It wasn't about romance—just fun.

Now? It's like there's an invisible scoreboard, and I'm definitely not winning.

This morning, kids were handing out chocolates and stuffed bears before the first bell even rang. By lunchtime, the cafeteria felt like some kind of Valentine's Day reality show. Couples were everywhere—hugging, giggling, sharing candy. Even people who *weren't* dating anyone had secret admirers and cards and stuff. It felt like love was everywhere...

And then there was me. With nothing.

Lilly didn't care, obviously. "It's literally just a marketing scam to sell bad chocolate," she said, peeling the wrapper off a heart-shaped lollipop someone gave her. (She still ate it, though.)

But Emma? She got *so much*. She literally was sitting with a pile of candy and cards and even a single rose. It was wild—she had even more than Jenny (who did not look happy about that!) But Emma looked totally thrilled to be getting all this attention.

And I was happy for her, really. But also... I don't know. It kind of sucked.

Not because I wanted flowers. Or a Valentine. Or anything like that. Well, maybe I did. But it was more because it felt like she was stepping into this world I wasn't part of yet. Like one second we were all just us, and now suddenly, people were getting flowers and talking about crushes and it felt like another shift I wasn't ready for.

And to make things worse, Emma was with her basketball friends and barely even looked at me as they all left school together to walk home.

I don't know what I expected. It's not like she was going to magically turn around with a chocolate heart and be like, "Hey, let's go back to how things were." But it still stung a little. I really thought after doing the whole presentation with her and Jenny that we were going back to normal, but I guess not.

When I got home, I sat in front of the mirror. I don't even know why—it's not like it was going to tell me anything I didn't already feel. But I just stared for a long time, trying to figure out if I was actually upset or if I was just being dramatic.

Then, quietly, I said, "You're not invisible."

I don't know if I believed it. But maybe if I say it enough times, one day I will.

Goodnight, Diary.

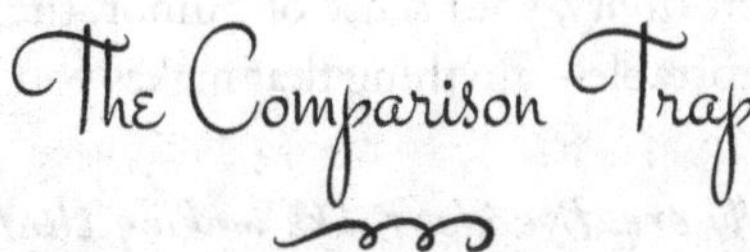# The Comparison Trap

When we compare ourselves to others, we forget how amazing we already are. Think about a time when you have compared yourself to someone else: Maybe it was about how they looked, how well they did in school or sports, or how popular they seemed. How did that make you feel? Write down a few words or draw a small doodle that represents that feeling.

I'm glad I remembered this worksheet Stella gave us the day we had the social media talk. Because after Valentine's Day, I can't stop comparing myself to everyone else!

REALITY CHECK

Now, take a step back and ask yourself: Did this comparison actually help me in any way?

No. Sometimes, like with schoolwork, it helps me get focused, but in this case, it just made me feel bad.

What strengths do you have that make you unique? It's time to own what makes you amazing! Think of one thing that is special about you—something that makes you unique. It could be your kindness, your creativity, your sense of humor, the way you make people feel comfortable—anything that makes you, *you*.

I have really creative ideas, like making that aquarium diorama, and I'm getting more comfortable sharing them

If you were your own best friend, what would you say to myself in that moment?

Just because you didn't get a bunch of random presents on Valentine's Day doesn't mean people don't like you. You didn't give any to anyone else either!

FLIP THE SCRIPT: RECOGNIZING YOUR SUPERPOWER

Take a moment to reframe a thought you've had before—how can you turn it into a kind and encouraging one?

- Instead of thinking *"She's so much better at this than I am,"* try saying: *"I'm proud of how hard I'm trying."*
- Instead of *"I wish I looked like her,"* say: *"I have my own beauty, and that's enough."*

Instead of thinking that it sucks that no one has noticed me but everyone is noticing Emma, I can think that just because people are clearly interested in her, that doesn't mean no one likes me.

POWER POSE + AFFIRMATION

Let's try it again, stand tall, take a deep breath, and say to yourself: "Being myself is my superpower." Because it is! No one else has your exact mix of talents, dreams, and experiences. The world needs *you*, just as you are.

Reflect: How does it feel to celebrate *yourself* instead of comparing yourself? Keep reminding yourself: "No one is me, and that is my superpower."

I did this in my mirror and I really did feel a little better. (Also, mom left me a silly valentine card on the desk next to the mirror with a little box of chocolates... that helped too!)

Reminder: You deserve the same kindness you give to others. Instead of comparing yourself to someone else, try seeing yourself through the eyes of a friend—someone who loves and believes in you. Everyone has strengths and struggles, even if they don't show them. You are growing, learning, and doing your best, and that's more than enough. Be gentle with yourself—your journey is yours, and that's pretty special.

February 16

Dear Diary,

The winter has been quite mild which has been nice for biking and walking to and from school. On the bike, there's something freeing about the way the cold air rushes past your face. It makes me feel like I can leave the stress of school behind, at least for a while.

After school today, I decided to ride over to Anna's. She doesn't live too far from the school, actually she just lives down the street from the park. Right now, she gets to be at home for a little while, and my mom told me as long as I am careful, share my location with her, and wear my helmet, I can bike to her house.

We haven't hung out much lately, but she texted me saying "Come over! I've got a surprise." Of course, I couldn't say no to that. When I got there, her mom had the kitchen all set up for baking: bowls, measuring cups, and a recipe pulled up on her tablet. I do love baking when I do it. But I don't do it super often.

"It's supposed to be easy chocolate chip banana cookies," Anna said, making air quotes around the word 'easy.' "But with me, you never know." We started measuring flour, mashing bananas and talking about my school mini-dramas and what's been going on with her homeschooling between laughing at our baking incompetence as she accidentally spilled sugar all over the counter. "I'm a walking disaster," she groaned, brushing sugar

186

off her sleeves. For a second, she looked upset. But before I could jump in and tell her how great she is, she quickly reframed, and said, "No, I am grateful to be in the kitchen regardless if I mess this recipe up, because in the hospital I can't bake."

I'm always amazed how Anna always catches herself when she speaks negatively. I can catch when other people do it and help to turn it around, but I'm not so good at catching my own negative thoughts (like that one!). It felt good to just be with her, doing something simple. While the cookies were in the oven, she led me to the basement. I hadn't been to her house before, and I was mesmerized by all the cool paintings they have on the walls down there—all really bright and abstract and fun. I could see how being surrounded by all of those happy colors maybe helps her stay positive! (Maybe I should repaint my room? I should ask Mom!)

"Okay, now for the real surprise," Anna said, holding up a pair of colourful paddles and a ball. "One of the nurses gave me this set to bring home since a bunch of the kids at the hospital have started to play pickleball in the community area. Even some of my friends in wheelchairs are playing, and they're really good —so I need to practice so I can win!"

I love her secret competitive streak. Anyway, the nurse told her this smaller pickleball set would be good to practice with. Even with the smaller setup than a full pickleball court, I still had to move a few things in her basement to make more space. I also didn't want her to trip on anything, she sometimes has a hard time catching her balance when she makes sudden moves.

At first, I was terrible. Way worse than her! I kept missing the ball or hitting it into the boxes in the corner and having to go dig it out. But Anna didn't care. She cheered me on every time I got a good hit and made ridiculous faces when she missed, just to make me laugh. By the time the cookies were ready, we were out of breath, our cheeks red from laughing and running around.

Sitting at her kitchen table, eating warm cookies, I realized how much I'd missed moments like this simple, messy fun. The thing is, I don't think I've ever thought of myself as someone who enjoys sports, or even just movement. I'm more of a bookworm type. Sports at school always feel so serious and competitive.

Before I left, Anna even said that I could probably come play with them at the hospital on the full pickleball court if I wanted to. She also said she really wanted to play with other kids our age, since pickleball is something she can do pretty well when she's feeling good. I remember her telling me a couple weeks ago how she wishes she could do half the things I can, and I guess I've taken that for granted. Anna sure doesn't let anything stop her (unless the doctors completely advise against something).

Riding home, I couldn't stop thinking about how much fun it would be to do something like this at school. I wonder if I could create a space where everyone could join in—even Anna! Maybe I'm getting ahead of myself, but I kind of like the idea.

February 18

Dear Diary,

Today, Miss Adler handed out this worksheet about kindness and compassion and how doing something kind for someone else can have this thing called the butterfly effect, where a tiny kind thing becomes a lot more kindness and compassion everywhere. I really like that idea... and it made me think even more about how I want to do something for Anna, and how fun it would be to have her able to play with a lot of kids. I told Mom and Dad about playing pickleball with Anna and how I might want to do something with a pickleball game, maybe get some kids at school to play in some way where Anna could be involved and not feel like she's being left out. Dad has actually been playing pickleball with friends a lot lately, so he has a bunch of extra paddles and balls and even a few nets.

Mom suggested that instead of trying to start a team or something long-term and competitive, we could put on a fun charity event at school to give proceeds back to Anna's hospital. She's always thinking about ways to raise money, since stuff like pickleball for the kids at the hospital and all the other activities the nurses do for the kids there are all funded entirely by donations. I guess when you're not the one in the hospital, you just don't think about stuff like that, but Mom is always there reminding me.

At first, it was just a casual idea. But we kept talking about it through dinner, and even after Jake got bored and asked to be excused, we kept talking, and Mom even started writing down ideas on a notepad. We were thinking it could be like a one-day mini-pickleball tournament with teams, snacks, and maybe even prizes. Mom said we could do decorations around the school, think of a name and even get the kids at the hospital to help out by drawing up posters for the games and raffles, if we have any. The idea of doing something like this where Anna could have fun and hang out with the kids from school and we could raise money for a good cause made me feel really good.

At the same time, it's kind of scary thinking this big. I've never organized anything like this before. I mean, I barely even like raising my hand in class. But thankfully, Mom has tons of experience with charity events and said she'd help. And Anna has shown up for me these past months even when she was the one who was feeling actually sick. She always finds ways to make me laugh, to listen, and to distract me when I'm stuck in my head. So, I guess I'm in. Let's see where this goes!

The Butterfly Effect: Compassion Towards Others

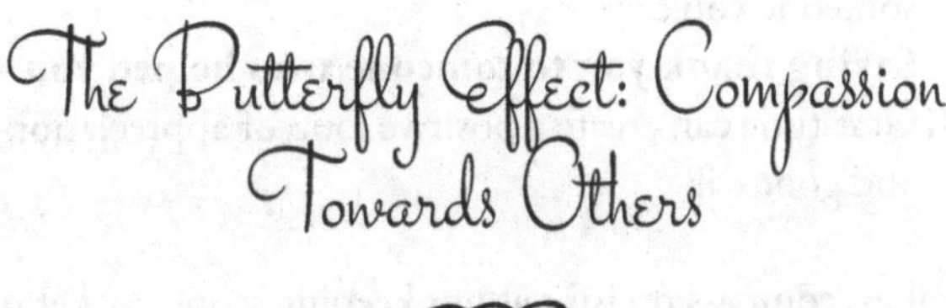

Compassion isn't just about big gestures—it's about the small things we do every day to show kindness and care. These small acts have the power to create a ripple effect, like the **butterfly effect**, where one small action can lead to much bigger changes in someone's day—and maybe even their life.

Think about it: When you show compassion, you never really know how far it might go. Maybe that smile you gave someone today made them feel seen. Maybe the compliment you gave someone made them feel more confident. One small act of kindness can spark a chain reaction that spreads even further than you could imagine, creating a kinder, more connected world.

Here are some ways to practice compassion in everyday life:

- **Helping a friend who's feeling overwhelmed** – Sometimes, just being there to listen or offer a hand can make all the difference.
- **Including someone in a conversation or activity** – You never know who's feeling left out, but your inclusion might make them feel like they belong.
- **Giving a genuine compliment** – Words can lift someone's spirits and remind them of their value.

- **Leaving a kind note for someone** – A little surprise kindness can brighten someone's day.
- **Listening when someone needs to talk** – Sometimes, just being a good listener can show someone you care.
- **Saying thank you to someone who helped you** – Gratitude can create a positive loop of appreciation and goodwill.

Remember, compassion isn't about keeping score—it's about making the world a little kinder, one small action at a time. These tiny acts, however small, can have a massive impact. You may never know how your kindness changed someone's day, but trust that it did.

Reflect: Think about a time you've shown compassion to someone else. How did it feel in that moment? How do you think it impacted that person, even if you didn't see it right away? By practicing kindness, you're part of a bigger, more beautiful shift.

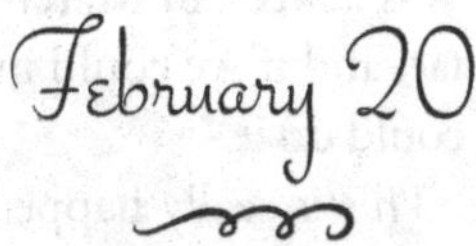

Dear Diary,

Today, I jumped out of bed excited to keep planning the pickleball event. Yesterday, Mom seemed a little nervous about me taking on too much and reminded me that I still have to time-manage my schoolwork and this, and didn't I want to spend more time with friends or try a dance class? But it's something I really want to do, so I guess we'll see how it goes. No time for negativity, I have a charity event to plan!

After talking to Mom and Dad about it, the first thing I did was text Anna about the idea, and just like I thought, she was over the moon thrilled to be part of this and thought it was a super cool idea to have proceeds go to support the hospital activities. I waited to tell Lilly and Emma at school, and when I did, Lilly practically jumped up and down when I told her. She was ready to get started on making posters for this and spreading the word. Even Emma, who I thought might be kind of indifferent, got really into it, probably because she's planning to run for student sports rep next year. She says this could also be a great way to get people thinking about how important sports and activities are.

She even came with me at lunch to talk to the current student sports reps, Claire, who had so many great ideas to add, and then instead of doing normal study hall, the three of us went into the administration office to run it by Mr. Davis, who is in charge of school council and activities. He said yes, and that they would look at the calendar and figure out when it could happen, but that he thought there was a week in March where there were no activities on the calendar, and if we could make it happen in that tight of a timeline, we could do it.

This is happening. This is really happening! I'm going to be facing my fear, just like I resolved to on New Years. Planning this whole huge thing that suddenly has involved way more people than I originally thought, and I'll probably have to speak on the school's announcements and talk to other kids about it, plus probably talk a lot during the event. Terrifying.

But it was also super exciting because it means that Emma and I will get to spend time together again, since she's keen on helping! It felt like the old days, having her by my side as we were talking to Claire and Mr. Davis.

Later this evening, I told Mom and Dad about how fast everything was already moving. We've gone from one little conversation a couple nights ago to now having a team of seven—me, Mom, Dad, Anna, Anna's Mom, Lilly, and Emma).

Mom was in full event-planner mode. "We should start making a timeline. Do you have a date in mind yet?"

I told her Mr. Davis said we could probably get gym time in about three weeks. Mom sighed at first because she thinks that isn't much time... But Dad nudged my head and ruffled my hair while saying "don't forget, have fun with it." Mom sighed even more at that, like she was thinking that Dad doesn't really understand what goes into planning something like this, and she does. But she didn't say it, I could just tell. We made eye contact and both started laughing at how clueless guys can be sometimes.

He's not totally wrong, though. This is fun. Right. No need to stress. This is about helping Anna, and making something good happen. I can do this... I think!!

I felt so good that I ended up actually giving myself a high five in my special mirror, congratulating myself for being brave and the gratitude I feel for having the support around me to help run this event... And it does feel good to think about helping others. I don't think I would have been able to do this at the start of the school year where I was constantly comparing myself and just trying to fit in. But now, I can.

February 23

Dear Diary,

So the countdown for three weeks is officially on! I got the okay from our school office this morning. I went to go talk to our school's secretary right when I got to school this morning. I was nervous... like, nervous to the point where I thought I was maybe going to be sick in the school bathroom.

I did end up in the bathroom but didn't throw up, thankfully. I did take some deep breaths, looked at myself in the mirror and said my affirmations... and I even gave myself a high-five in the mirror and did a quick power post. I really needed that. When I went into the office, I wasn't as nervous, and the secretary told me that Mr. Davis had okayed us holding the event on March 21, assuming Mom fills out all of the forms that he left for me.

After my conversation with Mom about how everything's moving so fast, I had another idea. I love baking, and Anna always makes baking feel like it's part of the fun. So, I thought, why not add a bake sale to our event? We could bake together, sell cookies, cakes, and other treats, and all the proceeds could go to the hospital activities too. Anna is just as much of a baker as I am, and it would be a way for us to share something we love while supporting a cause that means so much to both of us. I can already picture the table piled high with goodies—chocolate chip banana cookies, cupcakes, maybe even some banana bread. I know it would bring even more energy to the event, plus who doesn't love a sweet treat?

I texted Anna about the idea and she was all in—she was so excited to be part of the bake sale too, since that's something she knows she can help with no matter how she is feeling. I think it made her happy to have something that she can know she'll be able to do, since she's not always able to play pickleball. This felt like the perfect addition, and I can't wait to get started. I think this event is going to be even more amazing than I imagined, and it's really showing me that with a little courage, anything is possible.

I'm feeling a mix of excitement and nerves, but I'm ready for this challenge. I'm learning so much about planning, helping others, and even how to push through my own fears. I guess sometimes it's the little things that help you step up and make things happen. I'm grateful for Anna, my family, and all the people who are supporting me. Can't wait to see how this event turns out!

February 25

Dear Diary,

Today was a huge surprise. It turns out Jenny loves playing pickleball with her dad (and her parents are in the middle of a messy divorce, which explains why she's been so up and down this year). How did I find this out? I dove into planning the pickleball fundraiser with Emma and Lilly today, and had a surprise at lunch. As we were making a massive to-do list for the event, Jenny sat down with us and asked if she could help. I couldn't believe it, but she was so excited about it. She said she loved pickleball and really wanted to get involved and that her dad would probably love to help out too, and then she told us all about the divorce and how hard it's been. I was so surprised. Sure, we managed to be civil during the science project and even have a couple of fun moments together, but I never expected her to be this nice.

I guess when she was over at my house with mom's banana bread, that wasn't an act, that was her dealing with some really tough stuff. I can't imagine what it would be like if my parents were getting divorced. I don't think that makes it okay for her to be mean, but it does explain a lot. And I guess what it kind of reminded me of is the whole conversation Stella has had with us about comparisons. We're comparing ourselves and our lives to other people all the time, but we have no idea what's really going on in anyone's life. And maybe Jenny being mean wasn't even about me—it was about her all along.

Anyway, we brainstormed for a few minutes and Lilly had a genius idea: We should have a theme for the event about spreading kindness and compassion, based around the ideas that Miss Adler was telling us about in the . It's a little silly to call an event a Kindness and Compassion Pickleball Challenge, but we can still make that the theme.

We even listed some quick ideas. We could:

- Pair up experienced players with beginners (so no one feels left out)
- Hand out little "thank you" notes to volunteers
- Set up a "affirmation compliment station" where players can write kind messages on sticky notes

Pretty cool, right?

February 28

Dear Diary,

Today I had Anna, Lilly and Emma all over to my house to work on the event plans, and it was the first time I'd had us all in the same room where there wasn't anything else going on, like a movie or a basketball game. Weird to think of my worlds colliding! Actually, it's even weirder to realize that my worlds were separate, or that I have more than one world to begin with! I guess things really have changed since this summer when Lilly and Emma were my closest friends and we shared all of the same other friends.

Anyway, we were all just sitting at the dining room table working away. Anna was sketching up cupcake designs for the bake sale. Lilly was mapping out our social media posts and some art posters. Emma kept drifting off into her phone, and I think she was texting Jenny. I tried to get her input on the logistics, but she seemed very distant.

At one point, Lilly and Anna started talking about which teachers we should have go up against each other, since a few of them have signed up to play and we think it'll be really fun (and funny) to watch. But Emma barely chimed in.

Then, it hit me: I've been feeling left out with all of Emma's new friends, but maybe I have also been shutting Emma out, now that I see Anna so often. I asked Emma if she was okay. She looked surprised, and said she was just distracted. I told her it was fine and asked if she had any ideas for decorations or games. She brightened up and suggested we do a high five lane as people walk through to play the match or after the match. It was a great idea.

By the end, everyone had something to do and we were back to laughing together. I think I am learning that friends can connect in different ways, and that's okay. Emma's friendship with Jenny isn't my friendship with Emma, and my friendship with Anna isn't Emma's friendship with me, but they can both exist.

Wow! Planning this event is teaching me more than just organizing bake sales and pickleball.

March 5

Dear Diary,

It feels like spring is finally starting to show up! The sun's been out more, and the chill is starting to fade. It's been such a relief to get outside for walks again without wearing so many layers—there's something about that crisp air that feels like a fresh start.

Tomorrow is the annual book fair at school, and I can already feel the excitement buzzing. It's funny how something so familiar can still bring so much joy. Every year, I can count on the smell of freshly printed pages and the endless rows of books to get lost in. The best part? Getting to choose a new book to dive into, one that'll become my companion through the next few months.

I've been thinking about how much things have changed in the last year, but also how much has stayed the same. For some reason, the book fair always feels like a checkpoint, like a reminder of where I've been and where I'm going. A year ago, I would've worried about fitting in, about choosing the right book, about what everyone else thought. This year, I feel more at peace. I'm not saying I've got it all figured out, but I'm learning to appreciate the little things—the moments of calm and the people who make life richer.

Anyway, I can't wait to see what books I find tomorrow. I have a feeling this one might be special. Goodnight, Diary.

March 6

~∾~

Dear Diary,

The book fair was everything I remembered it to be—and then some. It was like stepping into a world of possibilities, with every aisle offering something new to explore. It's always so busy, with people from all grades milling around, and there's a certain magic about it. I even managed to pick out a book that's been on my wish list for months! It feels like such a small victory. It was one of those moments when it feels like a piece of the world is just for me.

Lilly and I ended up in a quiet corner with our new books, chatting about life and how our resolutions are going and how different our reading tastes have gotten since last book fair. I couldn't help but notice how much has changed in the last 12 months. It's still a work in progress but it feels like I've started moving in the right direction.

Speaking of progress, things have been going well with the pickleball charity event. The gym's booked, and everyone's been working on the details. We've been getting the word out about the event, and I can't believe how many people are getting involved and signing up. Lilly made a ton of posters and they look amazing—seriously, I might need her to make me some for my locker! It's crazy to think it's only been a couple weeks since I came up with the idea, and now we have a full team and a plan in place. I'm a little nervous, but mostly excited. I've been practicing my speeches—yes, plural. I have to talk during the event, and the idea of speaking in front of a crowd still freaks me out, but it's also a little thrilling too. I know I can handle things like this now. I'm learning that nerves are just part of it, and I don't have to let them control me.

But back to the fair. I know this sounds kind of silly, but after everything wrapped up, I spent a few minutes just standing in front of the bookshelves, thinking about how each of these books represents a journey, a story. And I think that's kind of what I'm doing right now—writing my own story, one chapter at a time. It's okay if things don't always go perfectly, and it's okay to not have everything figured out. But what matters is that I keep moving forward, keep learning, and keep making memories with the people who matter most. Maybe this is what Miss Adler meant when she handed out today's health class worksheet about celebrating small wins.

Celebrating Small Wins or Daily High-Fives

Write down a few small wins at the end of each day—whether it's speaking up in class, tried a new sport, or just got through a tough moment. Reflect on how far you've come and celebrate these steps forward.

1. Picking a book I truly wanted. I didn't worry about what others thought; I just picked what made me happy. That's a win!

2. Practicing my speech. Even though public speaking still scares me, I'm preparing for it instead of avoiding it. That's progress!

3. Reminding myself I don't need to have it all figured out: just like the books, life unfolds one chapter at a time. And I'm okay with that.

March 9

Dear Diary,

Spring break. No alarm clocks. No math tests. No pretending I understand group projects. Just me, my mismatched socks, and the kitchen pantry calling my name. Also—Mom signed me up for that weekend dance camp, which I didn't think about until Mom reminded me of it this weekend. It starts Thursday morning. It's supposed to be super chill, not super serious, and (her words) "perfect for curious hearts who like to move." I laughed when she said that, but honestly, I kind of love that.

I'm nervous though. I haven't danced in front of actual people since my disastrous attempts at ballet years ago. What if I totally blank or feel awkward? What if everyone else is already amazing and I just look like I'm flailing?

But Mom reminded me: "You're not going to impress. You're going to express."

She's full of those wisdom drops lately. Plus, dancing in front of anyone is just good practice for having to speak at the pickleball tournament. Speaking of that, I need to get to work because this week is going to fly by and it's less than two weeks away!

So yeah. Dance camp is happening. Three days. New shoes. Open mind. Let's see what happens.

March 11

Dear Diary,

Okay. My bag is packed. Water bottle, leggings, snacks (obviously), and a playlist in case I need to hype myself up in the car.

I'm feeling this mix of butterflies and buzzing. I've been so busy trying to get the schedule for the pickleball tournament sorted out and all the little decoration details worked through and coordinating with Lilly and Emma and Anna that I haven't had a lot of time to have nerves about camp, until tonight. I caught myself doing a little freestyle thing in the mirror before I got tucked into bed here and I didn't hate how it looked. Not that it looked good—but it felt good. I even gave myself a goofy little mirror thumbs up after. Silly stuff like that feels even better in my special mirror.

Also, I peeked at the camp schedule. There's hip hop, contemporary, and something called "groove flow"? No clue what that is, but it sounds like a yoga dance baby and I'm kind of into it. I don't know who I'll meet or if I'll even like it, but I am in this place where trying something new doesn't terrify me. I think all the charity prep has really helped with this.

Okay, maybe it still does make me nervous a little. Okay, a lot. But I'm going anyway.

Wish me luck.

March 12

～

Dear Diary,

My legs are jelly. My brain is a smoothie. And somehow—I totally loved today.

I almost backed out in the parking lot when we got there. Seriously. I sat there pretending to "check my phone" for like five minutes while people walked in with their duffel bags and effortless buns. But then one of the instructors literally danced her way across the lot and waved at me like we were old friends. Her name's Jules. She's like Miss Adler in a hoodie.

First class was hip hop, and I thought I'd be completely lost. But they broke it down step-by-step, and we got to make it our own toward the end. That was my favorite part—when we weren't all moving in perfect unison, but still in sync in a weird, messy, beautiful way. It reminded me of messing around with Anna doing goofy dances.

Because of that, I didn't worry about what I looked like. I just moved.

Also, I met a girl named Anika who's trying out dance for the first time too. We both admitted we were lowkey terrified but laughed through the whole warm-up. Instant friend vibes.

I'm so tired, but the good kind.

$$March\ 15$$

Dear Diary,

I'm already sad it's over. Today, the final day of dance camp, was all about expression. We did this free movement exercise where they played a song, turned down the lights, and let us dance however we wanted. No choreography. No rules. Just music and feeling and bodies moving in whatever way they needed to.

I didn't expect to cry, but I did. Just a little. It wasn't even a sad cry. It was more like... release. Like I gave my body permission to be seen for the first time in a long time.

Afterwards, Jules came up and said, "You've got something special. You move like you're telling a story. Keep listening to that." And I think I will.

I don't know if I'll become "a dancer," but I think I found a way to be in my body that doesn't feel like a battle. It feels like a beginning.

Mom was waiting outside with a smoothie and the biggest grin. She said I looked happy.

And I am. I sort of felt like I was far removed from my typical "life" this week. I didn't see any of my friends, and weirdly I kind of think I needed to just regroup, to work on event planning with Mom and to be completely invested in this dance camp.

But now, it's back to the real world. We only have a week to go for the charity event. Maybe I'll do another dance class or camp, but first, there's a lot of work to do!

March 16

Dear Diary,

Today, I swear my heart's still dancing. I thought I'd wake up sore and maybe a little over it—but nope. I woke up smiling. I've replayed that free movement session like a million times in my head. I don't think I fully understood how much I've been holding back—like I needed someone to say "go ahead, move how you want" to finally give myself permission. My morning power up routine was even more dance-y than usual!

And now I keep thinking... What else have I been scared to try just because I thought I wouldn't be good enough? It's kind of wild how just a few days can open up a part of you that's been sleeping.

I even caught myself humming one of the camp songs in the kitchen and doing a little spin while waiting for the kettle to boil. My mom laughed and said, "Looks like someone caught the dance bug."

I'm not saying I'm switching my whole life to become a dancer or anything. But now I know that moving my body can be about joy and not just performance or pressure. And that's huge for me.

Anyway, I've got a big week ahead. The charity event is getting real—like, happening-in-days real. I've got texts coming in, meetings with the girls, and a checklist growing by the minute. It's going to be a lot.

But after these last few days, I think I'm ready.

March 17

Dear Diary,

Time is flying by! I can't even explain how crazy it's been, juggling everything—school, my friends, this event... But the excitement is starting to outweigh the nerves.

Today, I just needed to sit down and write things out. It has been a whirlwind. Lilly's been really pushing last minute sign ups while Emma's been helping organize the schedule, which is a relief because I honestly had no idea where to even start with that. And then there's Anna. She's been giving me pep talks, making sure I stay focused, and of course, she's baking (and asking me to taste test new recipes, which I am *so* on board with).

Anna's mom is helping us with some of the supplies, and we're also making a whole bunch of treats together on the night before. It's going to be so much fun—and hopefully delicious!

Anyway, I've got a million things to do between now and next week. But I'm not going to stress— this is happening, and it's going to be great.

To do list:

- Finalize schedule and tournament brackets
- Check in with Anna & her mom about final list of bake sale items
- Ask about extra tables for setup

- Confirm music playlist (Lilly says she's on it)
- Remind volunteers of their shifts
- Pick up poster prints from print shop
- Make a thank-you speech... yikes!
- Pack emergency supplies: tape, scissors, Band-Aids (because... me)
- Write a reminder post for social media

I'll let you know how it goes.

March 18

~∞~

Dear Diary,

Three days to go! It's like everything has been building up to this moment, and now that it's almost here, I'm feeling a mix of excitement and nervous energy. There's still so much to do, but I'm trying to take a deep breath and remind myself that it's all part of the process.

Today after school was a blur of last-minute prep—finalizing the schedule, getting the decorations set up, and grocery shopping for the bake sale supplies with Anna's mom. I've also had a lot of support from everyone, which has made all the difference. Lilly and Emma are handling the posters and social media updates, and tonight, I'm working on my speech for the event. I never thought I'd be the one giving a speech at something like this, but I'm starting to feel a little more comfortable with the idea. It's still a bit intimidating, but I keep telling myself that it's okay to be nervous. I don't have to be perfect—I just need to be me.

Speaking of being me, something really clicked this week. As I've been working so hard on getting everything organized, I've realized this event is about so much more than just raising money —it's about connection. It's about coming together as a community to support each other, and it's about showing the world that we're all capable of making a difference, no matter how small we think our contributions are. It's about building something, making a difference, and showing people how important it is to support each other. Anna's hospital has given so much to her, and I want to help give back however I can. Plus, I think this event is a chance for everyone in my grade to come together, have fun, and maybe even realize that sports and movement are about more than just competition. They're about being alive, feeling good, and finding joy in the little things.

Hmm... That may be good to use in my speech!

The more I think about it, the more I see how much this event has impacted me personally. It's taught me about my own strength—about being able to step up and lead, even when I don't feel 100 percent ready. I've come to understand that even though it's scary to step outside my comfort zone, this is exactly where growth happens. And that's exactly what I'm going to do Saturday. I'm going to give it my best shot, not because I have all the answers, but because I believe in the cause, and I believe in my ability to make a positive impact.

Every little action—every poster Lilly designed, every schedule detail that Emma wrote out, every treat Anna and her mom baked—it all adds up to something bigger than we can see right now. Maybe we won't realize it immediately, but these small acts of kindness, dedication, and support will ripple out into the community, spreading positivity and encouraging others to take action too. Maybe someone will be inspired to organize their own event, or maybe someone will feel a little more confident in stepping up for a cause that matters to them. The point is, no matter how small our individual contributions seem, they all have the potential to make a lasting impact.

So, even though there's still so much to do, I'm reminding myself to embrace the chaos because it's all part of something beautiful. We're creating something meaningful, and I can't wait to see how it all comes together. We're showing up for each other and realizing that we can all make a difference, one small act at a time.

It's almost time. Here's to making it count!

March 19

⁓

Miss Adler has been trying to get us to do a daily gratitude practice for a while, and I think I'm ready to try it right now, while I'm feeling really thankful for a lot of things (and a little stressed out and need a boost). She says that gratitude isn't just saying thank you, it's about learning to notice the little things even on hard days. Regularly writing down a few things you're grateful or thankful for can help shift your mindset, build self awareness and bring more calm and joy into your life. So, I'll take a minute to reflect!

1. I am grateful for Anna's excitement. Her support and enthusiasm makes this feel even more real and possible. I love that we're in this together.
2. Lilly. Seeing her practically jump up and down made me realize how much others care about this too. I'm grateful for friends who bring the hype!
3. Emma's unexpected support. Even though I wasn't sure how she'd react, she's already thinking about how this event could help more people.
4. Claire's ideas. It means so much to have someone with experience guiding us. She's already helping make this feel more official.

5. Mom. Even when she sighs, I know she believes in me. Grateful for her wisdom and event-planning brain.

6. Dad's humour and encouragement. Only he would somehow bring the fact that he has a pickleball paddle collection up like that makes him somehow a cool dad. But he reminded me of the most important thing: have fun with it.

7. My own courage. A few months ago, heck even a few weeks ago, I wouldn't have dared to take this on. Now, I'm standing in front of the mirror telling myself I can do this. That alone is something to be grateful for.

8. The Power of a Team. I started this with just an idea, and now I have a whole group of people ready to help. That's something really special.

9. The Chance to Give Back. More than anything, I'm grateful for the opportunity to do something meaningful—for Anna, for the hospital, for everyone who will benefit from this event.

Just making this list made me feel so much more relaxed. Imagine I keep this list going and add to it every day...

March 20

Dear Diary,

The charity event is tomorrow, and I'm officially in full-on panickish mode. We baked our butts off yesterday after school and all the goodies are ready. Today, we set up the gym with the nets and tables. And tonight, I decided to take a break from all the craziness and just relax at home.

It's funny, though—when I'm at home with just my family, it feels like everything slows down. Like I'm reminded of who I really am at my core, not just the girl planning a big event now. I can just be Grace. The only thing is, I know Mom and Dad are proud of me for organizing the event, but sometimes I feel like they don't fully get what it means to me—I think they just see it as a small thing I'm doing for my class at school. They support me, of course, but I don't think they realize how huge it is to me. That kind of bothers me, but at the same time, it's a good reminder that it's okay if things don't go perfectly. I'll still be me.

Tonight, I was practicing my speech into my special mirror, which is my new go-to for when I want to feel really strong and powerful (I do it standing in my power pose!), and my brother kept interrupting me, asking why I was talking to myself. But instead of being really annoyed, I just laughed it off. He's so young, so of course, he doesn't get it. It was a little annoying, but it was nice to have something that grounded me in the chaos.

When I was done practicing and came out to join the family for a movie, my dad gave me a quiet thumbs-up from his chair, not saying anything, but I could tell he was proud. It's funny how he doesn't always say the words, but I know that's his way of showing he believes in me. My mom, on the other hand, couldn't resist offering feedback. "Maybe slow down a little on the first part," she said. "And don't forget to smile when you get to the good part." I smiled and nodded, but part of me just wanted to tell her I'd practiced this speech a thousand times in my head and already knew the points she was going to make. I didn't, though. Because she's my mom, and that's what moms do. And I appreciate that. (Most of the time.)

I also spent some quiet time with my dad in the backyard after the movie, right as the stars came out. We didn't talk much. He just sat there with me, which was exactly what I needed. Sometimes, I think we forget how much just being with someone means. He didn't have to say anything for me to feel like everything was going to be okay. I guess in that way, I take after him—I don't always need to say a lot to show I care.

Later, I caught a glimpse of myself in my mirror before heading to bed. I still can't believe I'm about to give a speech in front of so many people. But looking at myself, I reminded myself that I've got this. I've put in the work, I've got the support, and I have something important to share. I'm nervous, sure, but I know I'll be okay. I just need to trust myself and remember that I'm more than enough.

Right now, I feel like I'm exactly where I need to be—surrounded by people who love me, practicing the words that matter most. Wish me luck tomorrow!

March 21

Dear Diary,

Wow, what a day! The event was more than I ever expected it to be. We were playing pickleball all afternoon for the fundraiser, and I honestly didn't think it was going to be that much fun. But once everyone got into it, the energy was amazing. It was cool seeing everyone get so excited about the game, cheering each other on, and just having a good time. It was like the whole school came together for a good cause, and I was super proud of how everything turned out. It wasn't just about the game—it was about supporting each other, feeling good in our own skin, and giving back.

In the end, we actually stopped keeping score because everyone was just jumping in and playing against random people and Emma kept trying to write everything down but couldn't, so she just yelled, "I give up!" and tossed the scoreboard in the air. That got a big laugh, and no one seemed to mind... Not even Jenny, who was actually winning before the scores got tossed. She just laughed and went along with it, and honestly, she was so helpful all day. I haven't mentioned her a lot, but not because she hasn't been helping. She's helped a lot, but in a quiet way. She hasn't been stealing the spotlight or hogging credit, she just helped set up nets and tables and decorations behind the scenes.

It was a whole new side of her—one that I would like to get to know better.

Naturally, the bake sale was a huge hit! We had these amazing cupcakes and brownies, and the line was crazy the whole time. My mom also pitched in with a batch of cookies and she spent the whole time talking to people and handing out snacks. It was really fun to watch everyone come together like that: I didn't realize that she and Anna's mom have become friends too. The bake sale raised a ton of money, and I think everyone felt proud of how it all turned out.

Then, right in the middle of everything, I had this idea. I wanted to add a little extra spark to the event, so I decided to do a body appreciation moment. I felt like it would be nice to pause for a second and remind everyone how amazing they are, just as they are. But then, of course, I thought—why not take it a step further? So, I suggested a spontaneous dance break. I didn't know if anyone would actually join in, but the moment I said it, the whole vibe shifted. People lit up. As the event's official DJ, Lilly turned up the music and the whole gym felt electric. Everyone was moving, letting go of their nerves, and just having fun with it. It was such a good reminder that we don't have to take ourselves too seriously, and our bodies are made for fun and expression, not just for how we look.

After the dance break, we got back to pickleball, and the energy in the room was amazing. I noticed something—this butterfly effect was happening. People were smiling, high-fiving, and just being kinder to each other. It was like that little moment of dancing and body appreciation had set something in motion. Even the game felt more lighthearted, like we were all just happy to be there together.

But, as much as the day was full of good vibes, I couldn't help but notice that some of my friends weren't completely caught up in it. Emma, in particular, was quieter than usual towards the end. She didn't really join in during the dance party, and she seemed to be holding back the whole time. I get it—sometimes it's hard to be as confident as the moment demands. And while everyone else was vibing, she seemed like she was still struggling with something. I really hope she knows she's amazing just the way she is, even if she didn't feel like part of the crowd today.

And Anna—she looked like she was having so much fun! I was so glad she was there, and her mom, too. I could see her lighting up when she helped out with the bake sale, and I think her kindness and support made a big difference today. She's always so caring, and it was nice to see her be part of the event in such a big way. She was able to play a round of pickleball with me on her team, but I could tell it really tired her out. Still, no one else would have been able to pick up on that fact. She went back to manning the bake sale table with her usual swagger.

I'm just so proud of what we created. The pickleball, the dance party, the bake sale, and all those little moments of connection—today was everything I could have hoped for and more. It really showed me how the smallest actions can create the biggest waves. All it takes is one little moment to shift everything. I'll keep doing my part, sending out those positive vibes, and trusting that the ripple effect will take care of the rest.

March 22

Dear Diary,

I woke up this morning feeling like I had just run a marathon—my legs were sore, my arms ached, and I could barely drag myself out of bed. But it was the best kind of exhaustion.

Yesterday still feels like a blur of laughter, movement, and moments that will stick with me forever. It's like every piece of the day had its own little story, and together, they made something unforgettable.

I went over to Anna's and she was still buzzing about the bake sale, of course, and she made it her personal mission to find out exactly how much money we raised.

Naturally, as soon as the event was over, my brain started to think about what could be next. Anna suggested starting a "Random Acts of Kindness" week, where we'd each have to do something nice for someone else every day. She also wanted to start it as a viral social media trend, because she's Anna and she loves stuff like that. But it got me thinking about how to bring it to my whole class in real life.

I think the goal should be to do something small but meaningful, something that reminds us how much good happens in a day. That's when I remembered something I saw online—something about kindness jars. It was a tiny idea, but maybe it could turn into something bigger.

So that's the start of my plan. I'm going to research it a bit and maybe talk to Miss Adler. Because sometimes, the best way to end an amazing day is by figuring out how to make the next one even better.

March 25

Dear Diary,

I started searching online for the kindness jar idea that Anna and I talked about, and I found out that basically, the idea is that every time you do something kind for someone or receive kindness, you write it down on a little piece of paper and put it in the jar. Then, whenever you need a little reminder of how awesome people are, you can read through all the notes and feel good about the positivity around you. It sounded so simple, but it also seemed really powerful.

I could see this working for just me, but then I had an even better idea: Why not bring it to my whole class? Wouldn't it be cool if we all had a jar where we wrote down our kind moments? Maybe we could add things like helping someone with homework, complimenting someone's outfit, or just making someone smile. We could fill the jar with little acts of kindness, and at the end of each week, we could read some of them out loud. It'd be a great way to remind ourselves how much good there is around us, even on tough days.

So, I shared the idea with Miss Adler, and she loved it! She was totally on board and said it would be a fun way to build a more positive, supportive classroom vibe. I'm honestly so excited about this! I think it's going to be such a good reminder for all of us to focus on the good, especially when we're feeling down. I can already picture the jar sitting on our desk, overflowing with kindness notes. It'll be cool to see how it grows and how we all start looking for little acts of kindness throughout our day. It's not a big idea like a whole event, but sometimes the little things can make a big difference.

I'm really glad Miss Adler was on board with the idea, and I can't wait to start it. It's just one of those little things that can have a big impact. Plus, it'll be a fun project that helps everyone see how much kindness is out there, even when we're not looking for it. Here's to the Kindness Jar!

March 27

Dear Diary,

Miss Adler wanted me to explain the kindness jar idea to the class... and I screamed internally a little when she asked! I still get nervous, but after hosting the pickleball event and all the work I've been doing on being kind to myself, I kind of feel like I can step up to these moments.

At first, I was a little nervous telling everyone about the idea. What if people didn't take it seriously? What if no one wrote anything? But by the end of the first day, there were already a bunch of little folded notes in the jar. Miss Adler even read us a few. Someone wrote about a classmate helping them pick up their books after they dropped them. Another note said, "Maya let me borrow her extra pencil when I forgot mine." Even small things, like "Liam held the door open for everyone" or "Someone smiled at me when I was having a bad morning"—it was all in there. And it made me feel like everyone around me was just nicer and, well, kinder than I had realized.

The Kindness Jar

Whenever you think of something kind to say to yourself, write it down on a piece of paper and put it in the jar. When you're having a tough day, pull out a note and remind yourself of your worth. This helps to build a habit of positive self-talk.

April 1

Dear Diary,

Something kind of cool has started happening. All week, people were looking for kind things to write down. It was like, once we started paying attention to kindness, we saw it everywhere. And then... we all started doing more of it. Like, instead of just noticing kindness, we were actually trying to add to the jar.

Then another Friday came, and it was time to read some of the notes out loud. Miss Adler let us each pick one from the jar, and we took turns sharing them. Some made us smile, some made us laugh, and a few even made people blush (in a good way). It was honestly such a great moment—just sitting there, hearing all these little reminders that good things are happening all around us, even on days when it doesn't feel like it.

And you know what? The jar isn't even close to full yet. But I already know we're going to keep adding to it. I think we all realized something this week—kindness is kind of like a chain reaction. Once you start noticing it, you want to spread it. And that? That's pretty amazing.

Here's to week two of the Kindness Jar!

Dear Diary,

Today, Lilly, Emma, and I walked home together, but I knew something was really off with Emma. She was quiet, but in a weird way, like she wanted to say something but wasn't. I couldn't ignore it, even though she's been sort of strange with me the past few months. I nudged her shoulder and asked what was wrong. First, she hesitated. But finally, she let out a deep breath and told us she felt really off today. I glance at Lilly, and she looks just as confused and worried as I felt. "Like... tired off? Or something-happened off?"

Emma shrugged, tugging her hoodie tighter around herself. She said "Both." Then she looked super embarrassed, and finally admitted what really happened. At the pickleball event, partway through the day, she went to the bathroom and realized she had gotten her period.

Whoa. Lilly and I both stopped in our tracks. "I can't believe you didn't tell us!" Lilly said, looking hurt. "This is a big deal!"

Emma looked so uncomfortable and said she didn't tell us because didn't want us to make it a big deal... But it is a big deal! She's the first one in our group to get it! Emma made a face at me like "Lucky me." I can tell she doesn't mean it in a happy way. She looked embarrassed. Maybe overwhelmed. And suddenly, I got it—that was why she wasn't herself by the end of the event. It wasn't about the dance battle or the energy of the event. She was dealing with this and didn't know how to say it.

"Wait, what did you do when you got it?" Lilly asked. And I realized that none of us really knew what to say or do in this situation—trapped in a school restroom with your first period?

"It would have been a total nightmare," Emma said. "Luckily, Jenny came in and she had a pad in her locker so she went and grabbed it. No big deal."

I looked at Lilly and I could tell she felt the same thing I did: A little hurt that Emma told Jenny but not us. But I tried to see it from her perspective: She kind of had to tell Jenny, to get help. She's telling us now because she actually wants to.

Lilly said, "I say we should throw you a Period Party or something."

Emma groaned. "Absolutely not. But maybe a sleepover soon?"

We all laughed, and just like that, the weight in the air felt a little lighter.

April 8

Dear Diary,

I didn't think Emma having her period would be a big deal, after she told us about it. But I'm realizing now that things actually do feel different. Not in a bad way exactly, but it does seem like something invisible has changed and we're all pretending not to notice.

Emma's been acting a little weird this week. Not bad weird—just, I don't know, like she's trying really hard to be someone else? Like she's fast-forwarded a few years overnight. She started calling her hoodie a "cardigan" (even though it's totally just a hoodie), and yesterday she turned down ice cream because she "wasn't in the mood for sugar right now." Who even says that?!

When that happened, Lilly and I exchanged looks behind her back like: *Who is this person?!*

And today, when we were waiting for the bus, she pulled a book of poetry out of her bag. *Poetry*. And not even the kind we read in class. Like... old, dreamy love stuff. She kept nodding slowly like she understood it, but I swear I caught her flipping back a few pages to reread the same line over and over. She's trying to be mysterious or deep or something, I think. Or maybe she's just figuring things out.

I get it, kind of. Getting your period makes you feel like the world expects something new from you, like you're supposed to know how to be more adult overnight. Maybe she's just trying it on, like a new outfit. Seeing how it fits. I guess we're all going to go through this in our own weird, messy ways.

Still, I miss regular Emma. The one who snorted when she laughed too hard and always got chocolate on her chin. The one who never tried to "curate her aesthetic." (Yes, she actually said that today.)

But I also get it. Growing up feels strange. Like stretching into something that doesn't quite fit yet. I guess we're all becoming new versions of ourselves—and maybe, hopefully, still holding onto the old ones too. It's all weird, beautiful, awkward, confusing, exciting. But at least we're doing it together. Well, I hope together. There's been so many ups and downs with my friendship with Emma this school year. I just hope this new version of Emma is still my friend.

Dear Diary,

Emma is being her new quiet grown-up self, but I caught her smiling a few times, and I'd like to think she felt a little better about yesterday. She didn't say much about it, but when I gave her a little 'period pack' that I made for her (a super cute toiletries bag with pads and some Tylenol and a few little mini-chocolate bars), she said she loved it and tucked it into her locker like it was something important. That made me happy. I don't know—I guess it felt like a small sign that she knew someone had her back. That she wasn't alone.

But just when I thought Emma was the biggest issue in our little friend group, Lilly started going on about how she still hasn't gotten her period and how unfair it is. She was dramatic about it, obviously—said she was "literally being left behind" and that "her chest is still flat like a pancake." Her words, not mine. She said it loud enough that a couple people looked over, and I saw Emma kind of freeze for a second.

I wanted to say something, but I wasn't sure what. I get where Lilly's coming from—it's hard feeling like your body isn't doing what everyone else's is. But also... not everything is a race. I don't mind not having my period yet, though I also am now a little stressed about waiting for it to show up, considering

Emma's came right in the middle of a major event! What if I'd been in the middle of my thank you speech and got it?

Anyway, I hope tomorrow feels even better for Emma. And for Lilly too. Honestly, for all of us. This growing up thing is weird and confusing and beautiful all at once.

Dear Diary,

Mirror, mirror on my desk... Am I ever going to get breasts?! (LOL.) I stood in front of the mirror for a while today. Just staring. Not at anything specific really, just kind of hoping something would look different. Like I'd notice a sign or clue that I might finally be developing... you know, finally actually needing a bra! I even said that out loud, though I did burst into very immature giggles after.

But I just couldn't help feeling like this. Ever since Lilly had her outburst, I've been sort of thinking the same thing: When is it going to be my turn? Not that I want to get my period, exactly. But I do think it will make me feel more grown up, and maybe understand Emma better. Everyone keeps saying your body changes after you get it. But no one explains how. We tried to talk about it in health class with Miss Adler a few days ago—Lilly actually raised her hand and straight up asked about it—but the boys wouldn't stop laughing. So all Miss Adler really said was that getting your period means your body is learning how to take care of you in new ways. It is very hard to talk about, especially when guys are around. They were still snickering after class. Saying the word "period" out loud feels like a trap, like someone's going to roll their eyes or make a joke.

I asked Mom about hers and she said she didn't get hers until she went into high school. She even told me she felt really left out when her friends were getting theirs and she didn't have hers yet. I guess she's picked up on the fact that if I'm asking, it's because one of my friends got it. But still, that helped a bit. I guess I'm not late, just on my own schedule. I just feel like my body has been growing this year—I'm a couple inches taller—but no period, no need for a bra, no curves. It doesn't seem fair! Anyway, I just wanted to get that out.

Back to math homework now.

April 20

Dear Diary,

Maybe you saw this coming, Diary, but a year ago I never would've guessed that I'd be signing up for summer dance camp. Okay, technically Mom and I filled out the registration together on her laptop, but still—it's official. I'm going back.

Here's how it happened: This morning, I was in front of my mirror brushing my hair and kind of absentmindedly doing this little shoulder roll thing I learned at camp, and suddenly it just hit me. I miss it. Like, deep-in-my-chest miss it. The music, the weird warm-ups, the way my legs felt like jelly after and I love it anyway. And that feeling during the free movement part, like my body was telling a story I didn't know how to say out loud. I thought about it all day.

Then, when Mom got home, I blurted out, "Can I do the summer dance camp?" before I could chicken out. She grinned so wide I thought her face might break. Apparently, she was waiting for me to ask. And the best part? It's the same instructors, including Jules. There's even more "groove flow," which I'm now convinced is a yoga-dance baby and also my new favorite thing. I don't know if Anika's signing up too, but maybe I'll text her. Or maybe I'll just go and make new "terrified but trying anyway" friends like last time.

It feels weird to say this, but I think I'm actually proud of myself. I used to think bravery was like... this huge and dramatic thing. Running into a fire or standing up in front of the whole class. But maybe it's also clicking "submit" on a camp form. Maybe it's saying "yes" to something that makes your heart beat faster — the good kind, not the scary kind. Anyway, I'm writing it here so I don't forget: Today, I chose something just because it makes me feel happy inside.

Dear Diary,

Today was Mom's birthday, and we went out for dinner to this cozy Italian place she loves. It had twinkle lights everywhere and the kind of bread you could eat forever if no one stopped you.

Mom wore her fancy earrings—the ones she only puts on when she's feeling extra happy—and Dad kept sneaking little photos of her when she wasn't looking. It was actually kind of cute. Even my brother was less annoying than usual, which is saying something.

I made her a card with one of those pop-up flowers inside and wrote her a little note about how much I appreciate her always cheering me on, even when I don't totally believe in myself. She teared up when she read it and gave me one of those tight hugs that makes your whole body feel warm.

Also, I told her again how excited I am for summer dance camp, and she smiled so big and said, "I can't wait to see how you grow this summer." That made my stomach flip—in a good way. Like I'm starting to believe it too. Like maybe I really am growing. Not just taller (although, hello, my jeans are suddenly all ankle-length), but in other ways too. Like braver. A little more me.

I caught myself dancing down the hallway tonight when I

thought no one was looking. But then my brother yelled, "Nice moves!" from the bathroom and I almost died.

Anyway, it was a good day. Not just because of the pasta (which was amazing), but because I felt... like maybe I'm not waiting for something to change anymore. I'm already changing.

May 1

Dear Diary,

So, last weekend at Mom's birthday dinner, I felt confident in this dress I hadn't worn in a while. And then this morning? Not so much. It's weird how fast that can switch. One minute you're fine, the next your brain is being mean about your reflection. So instead of spiraling, I decided to write it out.

As I looked in my mirror today, I did try to remind myself of something important: My body is changing, and that's okay. It's supposed to. I'm not going to look like I did last year, or even a few months ago. And I'm not going to look like the girls I see online either and that's okay too.

I'm still learning to accept that some days I might feel good about myself, and others not as good. What matters is that I'm being nicer to myself along the way. Even if I don't totally believe it right now, I know that I'm more than just how I appear.

I'm trying to see my body for what it can do instead of just how it looks. It lets me run around, bike to school and dance with my friends. It's strong enough to keep up with all of that. That's something to be proud of, right?

So maybe self-acceptance isn't about loving every part of myself instantly (because let's be real, that's hard). It's more about being kind to myself when I have those days when I don't feel great, and remembering that it's okay not to look like anyone else. I'm still figuring out what self-acceptance means to me, but I know it's a journey, and I'm learning to be patient with myself. Here's what I've been thinking about lately: Maybe it's more about being patient, understanding that I'm still growing, and learning to treat myself with a little more kindness every day. I think that's a good place to start. I'm me, and that's my greatest superpower.

May 3

Dear Diary,

Today was Emma's birthday—I always remember since it's close to my mom's!—and she invited Jenny and all of her little inner circle to her party. Honestly, I was kind of dreading it. I always get nervous for birthday parties, especially when I don't know everyone there. I keep thinking, what if I pick the wrong gift? What if it's something they don't even want? Or worse, what if I don't fit in?

And then there's Jenny. I mean, we've been getting along and I know she's been getting closer with Emma. We made progress in the winter, but after the pickleball tournament, she kind of went back to being her normal self. Not outwardly mean to me, but not nice either. So, yeah, I wasn't exactly looking forward to spending time with her, especially with her little group of besties.

But when I got there, it was actually... kind of normal? Jenny wasn't acting all superior or making any sarcastic comments. She was quieter than I thought, just kind of hanging out with Emma and the others. It was like I was seeing a different side of her, and honestly, I didn't know how to feel about it.

Emma seemed really happy to have Jenny there, and I get it, they've been getting a lot closer lately. I guess that's how things go, but it made me feel a little weird. Like, what if I am actually being replaced? It's not like I want to be Emma's only friend (with Lilly, of course), but I don't know how to fit in with this new dynamic.

I tried to just focus on having fun and not stressing about everything, but it was hard. I didn't talk to Jenny much, but when we did a silly synchronized dance challenge, I saw her laugh for real, not like she was just pretending to have fun. To be honest, I still don't really know what to make of her.

I don't know. Maybe next time I'll feel a little less nervous about parties. Or maybe not. But at least I survived this one.

May 4

Dear Diary,

I woke up thinking about yesterday, and honestly, there was something that's been bugging me all day. I didn't really realize how much until I had some time to sit with it. I thought I was fine right after the party, but now I'm not so sure.

It was the way Jenny kept actually looking at me. When I tried talking to Emma about something, Jenny rolled her eyes and gave me this look, like she was already annoyed with me before I even said anything. It wasn't even that big of a deal, but it stuck with me.

I'm not sure why it bothers me so much. I know Jenny can be a little... harsh, but I didn't expect it to feel like this. Maybe it's because I've been trying really hard to get along with everyone, and it felt like she was completely shutting me out. Like I wasn't even worth noticing.

And then there's Emma. She didn't even seem to notice what was going on. Maybe she didn't see it, or maybe it just didn't seem like a big deal to her. I hate feeling like I'm being left behind, like things are changing, and I'm not sure where I stand anymore.

I don't want to feel like this. I just want things to go back to how they were before—when it felt easier.

Maybe I'm overthinking it. Oh, and I ended up texting Lilly.

I didn't tell her everything, but I guess I needed to talk to someone who gets it. I just said I kept feeling left out by Emma and Jenny. It felt good to get some of this off my chest with her, just like it feels good to get all of this out into you, Diary. Keeping you by my bedside is definitely a good idea, especially for nights like tonight when I can't sleep and I just need to write things down to clear my head.

$$May\ 8$$

Dear Diary,

Miss Adler was talking to us today about how we all have something that makes us "shine," even if we don't always see it. I don't really know what mine is yet. Sometimes I feel like other people sparkle more than me, like they've already figured out who they are and how to show it. I'm still learning what I like, what I'm good at, and what makes me feel alive. But maybe that's okay. Maybe part of shining is just being curious enough to look for the light.

When I looked in the mirror after school today after I had changed into comfy clothes for movie night with Mom, Dad and Jake, I tried to see more than just my face or what I look like. I stood there for a second longer than usual, brushing my hair and wondering what it would be like to see the whole me: to actually really see my strengths, my dreams, the things that make me excited, even if I don't talk about them out loud. Not just the outside stuff, but the spark underneath, the stuff that lives under the surface of me like a spark waiting to grow. Miss Adler says the seed is already inside us. It just takes a little time (and maybe some brave questions) to notice it.

So I'm going to do the SHINE exercise that she gave us, which might help me figure out what makes me, me... not the person I think I'm supposed to be. I know it won't give me all the answers. But if I've learned anything this year, it's that I am ready to learn more about who I am.

But on to movie night! Jake's already picked the movie. It's going to be a kid one, but I'm okay with that. There's a chance we might even do a backyard bonfire after. S'mores are my actual weakness, even if that's a little immature. Jake always burns his marshmallows to a crisp (on purpose—he says burnt is better), and I always try to get mine golden brown, even though it takes forever and a lot of skill. We haven't been able to have a bonfire this year because of the weather and Dad not having time to get one going, and I'm excited for it.

How Do You SHINE?

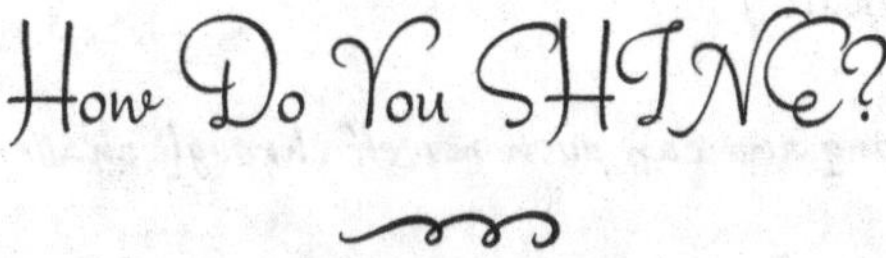

It's time to find what makes you SHINE!

- S – Strengths: Identify your unique strengths and qualities. What makes you shine?
- H – Hopes: Reflect on your aspirations and goals. What are you striving toward?
- I – Inspiration: What inspires you and keeps you motivated? Who are your role models?
- N – Needs: Recognize what you need to thrive— whether it's support, rest, or new opportunities.
- E – Empowerment: Take action to step into your power. What's one thing you can do today to embrace your shine?

Let's find out how you shine!

S – STRENGTHS

- **Prompt:** What are your unique strengths, qualities, and talents? Think about what you're really good at, whether it's sports, creativity, kindness, or something else.

251

- **Reflect:** Write down at least three strengths that make you proud of yourself. How do these strengths help you in your everyday life or in your goals? (*Example:* I'm a good listener and always make people feel heard.)

I'm strong and can push myself through challenges.

H – HOPES

- **Prompt:** What are your biggest dreams and aspirations? What do you hope for yourself in the future?
- **Reflect:** Write down one or two big dreams you have for your future. These could be related to school, sports, personal growth, or relationships. How do you envision yourself achieving them? (*Example:* I hope to run a marathon and feel strong while doing it.)

I hope to become a more confident speaker and share my thoughts with others.

I – INSPIRATION

- **Prompt:** Who or what inspires you? It could be a person, a book, a song, or even something you see in the world.
- **Reflect:** Who is your biggest role model, and what qualities do they have that you admire? What inspires you to keep going, especially when things get tough? (*Example:* Greta Thunberg inspires me to stand up for what I believe in.)

My mom inspires me because she works hard and never gives up, no matter the challenge.

N – NEEDS

- **Prompt:** What do you need to feel your best? This could be physical, emotional, or social needs.
- **Reflect:** Think about what helps you feel supported and at ease. Are there things you need to ask for more of, like rest, encouragement, or a break from social media? (*Example:* I need time to relax and recharge after a busy week.)

I need to ask for more help from my friends when I feel stressed.

E – EMPOWERMENT

- **Prompt:** How can you take action to step into your power and shine? What is one thing you can do today to feel more empowered?
- **Reflect:** Write down one action that can help you feel stronger, more confident, or more aligned with your goals. It could be something small, like speaking up in a class, or something bigger like setting a boundary with someone. (*Example:* I will remind myself of my strengths every morning to start my day with confidence.)

I will speak up in class today and share my thoughts, even if I feel nervous.

REFLECTION:

Once you've filled out the SHINE exercise, take a moment to reflect on what you've written. How does it feel to recognize your strengths and think about what empowers you?

This was really helpful reminding me that even though I have a lot I want to work on, I've already come so far. And I can do so much!

$$May\ 12$$

Dear Diary,

Lilly was acting kind of moody again today. She's still joking about being the "last to develop" and stuff like that, but today it really didn't sound like a joke. It is kind of strange how something your body doesn't do yet can make you feel invisible. I didn't realize growing up could be so complicated.

Even a few months ago, none of this was really taking over lunchtime talk, and now we're all rushing to want to see our bodies change just because other people's have. But then, we don't even fully appreciate it when it does, because seeing girls in our class get their periods and start talking about buying different bras seems exciting at first, but then not so exciting. Like there's this pressure to want those things, but when they actually happen, you're supposed to just know how to deal with it all.

Like there seems to be all these hidden rules no one really explains:

If your chest grows, don't talk about it too much, but also, don't act like you don't notice it. If you get your period, congrats, you're in the "club," but don't make a big deal out of it or it's weird.

If your hips get wider, or your skin breaks out, or your thighs touch, pretend you're fine, even if you're stressed about it. And also, you should be secretly working to fix it because it's not okay.

It's like there's this invisible script we're all supposed to be following, but nobody actually knows who wrote it or how to say the lines. And also, it's a terrible script and I want to throw it out!

And honestly? I'm kind of tired of pretending I know what I'm doing.

May 15

Dear Diary,

In health class today, Miss Adler had a talk with us about what "healthy" actually means today. It wasn't the usual "eat your vegetables and don't eat chips" kind of stuff. She asked us "what makes you feel fueled?" Not full. Not guilty. Not following what others are doing. *Fueled for you*. Like your body and brain are ready to do the things you care about. She said something that I wrote down right away in my planner, "Being healthy is less about following rules and more about finding balance. It's about listening to your body and showing it respect."

We talked about how balance can look different for everyone. That eating enough, getting rest, moving in ways that feel good, and letting yourself enjoy those snacks that sometimes are deemed "unhealthy" without spiraling is actually part of taking care of yourself. That real health isn't about looking a certain way, it's about functioning, feeling strong, being present and being kind to yourself when things don't go "perfectly."

It reminded me of some of the stuff we learned about self-compassion, actually. So after class, I went online and started looking up more about it. Total nerd stuff, but it was really cool! Turns out, self-compassion is actually really good for us:

- It helps improve body image and body appreciation (even when our bodies are changing).
- It lowers anxiety and makes us better able to handle things like stress and rejection.
- It helps us eat more intuitively, which means paying attention to how food makes us feel, not how it looks.
- It leads to healthier friendships (because we're not constantly comparing ourselves).
- It helps us cope better with tough stuff, like getting our periods, switching schools, or drama with friends.
- And most of all, it teaches us we are worthy, even when we mess up, feel awkward, or don't "fit in."

So yeah. Self-compassion equals more fuel, less pressure. And I guess "healthy" isn't one-size-fits all. It's like learning to be on your own team instead of working against yourself all the time. Pretty cool!

May 20

Dear Diary,

I hung out with Anna today, and we started talking about summer plans. It was nice just to chill together and talk about what we want to do when school's out—in addition to dance camp, of course. Anna's always so positive and has all these ideas for fun things to do, and I love hearing her plans because it gets me excited too.

We're thinking about going to the beach, playing pickleball with people regularly, and definitely checking out the new ice cream place in town. Honestly, the idea of summer sounds so freeing right now. I just want to spend time with the people I care about.

It's also nice to know Anna's got my back. She was the first one to say that we should have a summer bucket list, and we're both going to write it together. I think it'll be fun to look back on it at the end of the summer. Some ideas I already have:

- Picnic at the park
- Learn how to make friendship bracelets
- Go to the beach at sunset
- Movie marathon day
- DIY spa day
- Pickleball tournament at the park

A Letter to Me: My Compassionate Self

Writing a letter to yourself can feel silly at first, but it's a powerful way to practice self-compassion and to help yourself navigate hard moments. You can use this exercise anytime you need it, but take time now to practice writing a letter like this so you're ready when you need it next!

Practice writing a compassionate letter to yourself:

- Imagine you have a best friend who always supports you: What would they say to you if you were feeling down or struggling with something?
- Write yourself a letter using kind and encouraging words, just like a best friend would.
- You can start with: "Dear [your name], I want you to know..." or "I see how hard you try, and I want to remind you..."

SOME OTHER PROMPTS TO GET YOU STARTED:

Acknowledgment & Appreciation:

- Dear body, I want to thank you for...
- One thing I appreciate about you is...
- I recognize that you help me every day by...

Apology & Forgiveness:

- I now realize that when I said/did ___, it was unfair to you because...
- I'm sorry for the times I have...
- I forgive myself for...

Commitment to Kindness & Respect:

- Moving forward, I will try to treat you with more kindness by...
- Instead of being critical, I will remind myself that...
- I promise to take care of you by...

Reflection & Compassion:

- If I were speaking to a friend about their body, I would tell them...
- If my body could talk back to me, I think it would say...
- One way I can show my body compassion today is...

May 25

Dear Diary,

Today, Miss Adler talked about writing letters to ourselves again, but not just any letters, self-compassion letters. Instead of letters like we did at the start of the year where we were writing to ourselves a year from now to reflect on our goals, she explained that we should write to ourselves like we're our best friend, offering kindness and encouragement, especially on tough days.

We wrote the letter in class today. I found it kind of weird at first, but once I started writing, it felt good to say things to myself that I usually only say to other people. I wrote about how I'm proud of myself for trying new things lately—like dance camp— and the charity event. But I also wrote about how I need to remember it's okay to not be perfect. It's okay to have days where things don't go right or I don't feel great, but I can still be kind to myself.

Here's mine:

Dear Grace,

Hey, you. I know you've spent a lot of time wondering if you're enough. If you're saying the right things, doing the right things, being the right version of yourself. But here's what I want you to know—you are already enough, just as you are.

You don't have to be the loudest person in the room to be heard. You don't have to be perfect to be worthy. You don't have to have it all figured out to be deserving of kindness—including from yourself.

This year, you learned a lot. About friendships. About showing up for others and for yourself. About what it means to be strong—not just the kind of strong that pushes through no matter what, but the kind that allows softness, too. The kind that forgives. The kind that says, "I'm learning," instead of, "I should have known better."

And yeah, you still have moments where you doubt yourself. But instead of letting them define you, you're learning to meet them with kindness. To look in the mirror and see you—not just the things you wish you could change, but the things that make you you.

So, here's my promise:
I will be kind to myself.
I will celebrate my wins—big or small.
I will speak to myself the way I would to a friend.
I will remind myself that I am still a work in progress, and that's okay.
And when I forget, I'll come back to these words.
Because no matter what, I am enough.

With love,
Me

June 3

Dear Diary,

Today was a long day. Mom had me help her deep clean the house because it was the long weekend. We were moving furniture, dusting every corner, and sorting through old stuff. While we were working, I was reminiscing about how I'd found the mirror in the attic. It made me think back to how much this school year has been a new journey for me, how it's kind of wild just how much has changed. The mirror has been with me through this whole year reminding me to celebrate what makes me me and not just what changes on the outside.

I've been updating Mom on my friendship with Emma, and how she's been quieter, and sort of struggling with all the changes. How she kinda smiles less, and how our friendship feels sort of different. I mentioned how she got her period recently and how she's been feeling weird about it. Mom said that might even be harder for her because of sports. Like, with basketball starting up again in the fall, maybe she's already thinking about how all of this might affect how she plays, what she wears, and how she feels in her body on the court.

Sometimes things we don't even say out loud are still swirling around in our heads. And that was when I realized something big. I realized that maybe Emma needs the mirror now. Maybe it can be a little reminder that she's still herself, no matter what changes she's going through. That kindness—the kind I have been learning to give myself this year—might be exactly what she needs. I'm a bit nervous about giving it to her, though. She was joking around when I first told the girls I found this mirror and showed them a picture of it and the sticky note on it. What if she thinks it's weird, and our friendship can't handle that? But if this mirror can help Emma see what I see, that she's enough, just as she is, then it's worth taking the chance.

June 6

Dear Diary,

The last day of school. Summer is officially here! After we dropped Lilly at her house, Emma and I walked home from school together, and I made her come inside just for a minute so I could grab my mirror. I had tied a pretty ribbon around it, and used tape to make sure the sticky note would stay in place as I passed it on.

Emma blinked at it when I handed it to her. And she didn't respond with much enthusiasm, she just said "Uh... thanks?" I almost panicked and took it back, but I told her that I thought she could use it right now. I told her that whenever I looked in it, it reminded me that being me was enough. And that she could look in it and remember that even though things are changing, she is still Emma. The same Emma who crushed her math test last week. The same Emma who makes us all laugh at the worst possible moments. The same Emma who is awesome, with or without this whole period thing, with or without other friends, with or without growing up.

For a second, she just stared at me. Then, slowly, she smiled—and it was a real one this time. She said thank you, and kind of hugged the mirror to her chest.

I don't know if Emma will understand it yet, but that mirror? It's not about what's on it. It's what's always been inside of her.

Maybe she'll figure out that the way she talks to herself is the real reflection. It doesn't matter what mirror she's looking into. This will stick with her no matter where she goes. I know that because now any mirror I see has become my magic mirror. I hope she knows that her uniqueness—and all of our uniqueness—is what makes us, us. And that's our greatest superpower in the world. Why would we want to be like anyone else?

My Mirror Contract

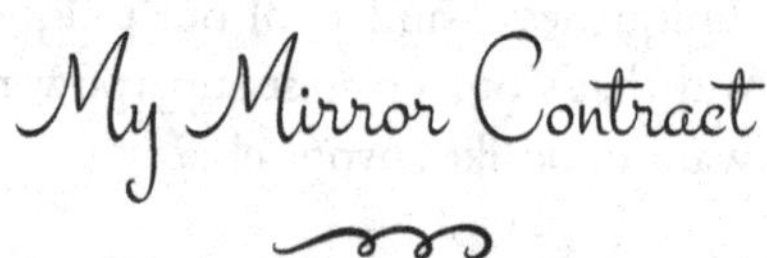

I, _________________________, promise to treat myself with kindness every day. I commit to:

Speaking Kindly to Myself: I will use gentle and encouraging words when I talk to myself, just like I would with a friend.

Appreciating My Unique Qualities: I will celebrate what makes me special, and remember that everyone is different in wonderful ways.

Forgiving My Mistakes: I understand that everyone makes mistakes. I will learn from them and not be too hard on myself.

Taking Care of My Body and Mind: I will rest when I need to, nourish my body to flourish, move my body in ways that feel good, and do things that make me happy.

. . .

Asking for Help When I Need It: I know it's okay to ask for support from family, friends, or teachers.

Standing Up for Myself and Others: I will be brave and speak up if I or someone else is not being treated kindly.

Practicing Gratitude: I will notice and appreciate the good things about myself and my life.

I promise to do my best to treat myself with kindness and respect every day.

When I forget, I will gently remind myself and try again.

Signed: ______________________________________

Date: ______________________________________

Acknowledgments

There's no way this book would be in your hands without a whole crew of incredible people.

First, to my family and friends—thank you for believing in this work (and in me) even when I doubted both. Thank you for being there through the highs and lows, and for cheering me on every step of the way. Your love, encouragement, and constant presence have held me steady. I couldn't have done this without you.

Professionally, I'm forever grateful to the researchers, advocates, and visionaries whose work laid the groundwork for this book's heart. To all my mentors and the leaders in this space—thank you for the knowledge, passion, and purpose you bring to this work. I continue to be inspired by the pioneers of this field and look forward to building new collaborations with you across the globe. A special thank you to Dr. Catherine Sabiston, Dr. Zali Yager, and Dr. Eva Pila—your mentorship and support have shaped not only my research, but the person I've become through it. And to Dr. Kristin Neff, thank you for giving us the language and science behind self-compassion—your work helped me rewrite not just these pages, but my own inner voice.

To my colleagues and collaborators I get to work with every day—I am endlessly inspired by you all and so grateful for the opportunity to learn and grow alongside you.

To Molly Hurford, the best publisher and writer I know—thank you for always listening to my big ideas and making things happen. Words will never fully express how grateful I am that we're doing this together. Your passion for getting this important work out there, combined with how much you genuinely care, inspires me every day. Everything you're building with Strong

Girl Publishing is incredible, and I'm so grateful to be part of this crew as we keep bringing more stories to life. You're a true inspiration—someone who's not just doing it all, but doing it with heart.

To Lisa Baldwin, your thoughtful edits and incredible suggestions helped shape this work into what it is. Your creative spark and ability to help me see a vast range of perspectives never went unnoticed. Thank you for bringing such care, clarity, and vision to every step of the process.

And of course, to the organizations near and far doing the real work every day—thank you. A special shoutout to a few I've had the privilege of working alongside and that are close to my heart; Girls Forward Foundation, The Embrace Collective, and Big Brothers Big Sisters. And to all those I haven't crossed paths with—I see you, and I hope we meet along the way.

Thank you for holding the mirror up, for every girl who needs to remember how enough she already is.

Emma's Story is Coming Soon!

You met Emma in Grace's story—the confident one, the sporty one, the girl who always seems to have it together. But what if being "the athletic one" came with a pressure she's only just starting to name?

In **Book 2**, we step into Emma's shoes—literally. She's navigating a new sport season, where things aren't feeling as fun as they used to. Between the rollout of white shorts in the new uniform (who approved that?) and whispers about bodies, performance, and who looks "fit" enough to lead, Emma's world starts to shift.

And when a new teammate joins who doesn't fit the usual mold, Emma starts questioning the unspoken rules of sport—and whether she really wants to keep playing by them. **You'll find:**

- The real-life highs and lows of team sports
- Loving the grind, but learning when to rest
- Uniform discomfort (hello, white shorts!) and body image thoughts that sneak up at game time
- Trying to be the role model—even when you feel like you're falling apart
- Standing up for yourself and others, even when your voice shakes

Book 2 is for every girl who's ever felt strong and insecure, powerful and uncertain—sometimes in the same breath.

Because being an athlete doesn't mean you're invincible— it means you can be tough, talented, and still have tough days.

Follow along with the Mirror Diaries at: **StrongGirlPublishing. com/Mirror**

About the Author

Vanessa Coulbeck is a researcher focused on body image, self-compassion, and physical activity among girls. She has worked with national and international organizations to develop educational tools and evidence-informed strategies that promote body acceptance, self-compassion, and inclusive physical activity. Vanessa's work bridges academic, nonprofit, and innovation sectors, with a focus on real-world impact and well-being. She has presented her work at national and global conferences, including the World Health Organization's Physical Activity Congress, the European Congress of Sport, and has contributed to discussions and shared her work at the United Nations Headquarters. She continues to lead and advise on innovative projects that empower girls and women in movement spaces.

Beyond her work, Vanessa loves to travel, explore new cultures, and discover hidden gem cafes. Time with friends and family, sunset walks, and staying active through nature hikes, pilates, and yoga flows are all part of her rhythm. She enjoys hosting themed dinners and cozy gatherings with loved ones, and is often found cooking or baking something new. A big sports fan, she finds joy in watching games and the passion that brings people together. Vanessa also volunteers with organizations and events that align with her passions and values.

<h1 style="text-align:center">More from Strong Girl Publishing</h1>

Shred Girls Series

Lindsay's Joyride
Ali's Rocky Ride
Jen's Bumpy Ride
Lindsay and the Curse of Gemini Lakes

Other Titles from Strong Girl Publishing

The Strong Girl by Molly Hurford
In Defense of Big Dreams by Mackenzie Myatt
Running as Fast as We Can by Molly Hurford
Sprinting Through Setbacks by Micha Powell
Best Day Ever Journal by Rachel Pageau
The Athlete's Guide to Sponsorship by Molly Hurford

Find more books like this at StrongGirlPublishing.com

The worksheets and exercises in this book are evidence-informed and draw upon research across several key themes: body appreciation and functionality, self-compassion and mindfulness, positive psychology interventions, and social-psychological strategies.

There are so many incredible organizations, websites, and resources out there doing meaningful work to support girls in this space. Because the research is constantly being updated and expanded, we've created an evolving reference page online so you can always find updated links and explore more. Head to StrongGirlPublishing.com/mirror or use the QR code below to access a list of references, bonus materials, supportive spaces, tools, and initiatives.

* 9 7 8 1 0 6 8 8 3 0 2 7 3 *